IRIS ALL IN

AN
IRIS WINTERBEK
--ADVENTURE--

IRIS
ALL IN

NANCY BARTLETT

Iris All In
Copyright © 2020 Nancy Taylor Bartlett
All rights reserved.

Cover Design by Ana Grigoriu-Voicu
www.books-design.com

This is a work of fiction.
Names, characters, places, and incidents either are the product of the author's imagination, or are used fictitiously. Any resemblance to actual persons, living or dead, events, or locales is coincidental.

For the true friends who join us in adventure

PROLOGUE

Gloria Trammel looked into the camera, cocked her head, and smiled for all she was worth. Which was a lot.

"Hello, my Glorious friends! Welcome to today's episode of Gloria!"

She moved slowly across the room, beckoning her audience to follow.

"I have such a fabulous surprise for you today. We're going to make any of your friends who are silly enough not to follow my show, ungodly jealous." She laughed. "But you who are truly smart and beautiful are about to reap the rewards of your loyalty, because I am the first to receive the new season's nail varnishes from Raffaella Revello! Today I'm going to reveal this glamorous rainbow for your nails, along with a very special offer. When you see these colors, I know you will want each and every shade. Trust me, your friends are going to swoon with envy." She pursed her ruby-red lips and saucily winked into the camera.

"But first," Gloria said, as she sat down behind her beloved Cassoni De-symetria desk, running her fingertips over the rich

1

leather top, "remember, today is my Local Glory Brunch at Blackfish Casino. I know many of you Seattle area viewers are planning to join me. The main event is sold out, but the casino welcomes any of you who have recently found my drop-dead gorgeous channel to be there as last-minute guests. We'll meet in the hotel lobby after brunch for photos and gifts. So see you later this morning. And for those of you who don't live in Washington state, I'll be coming to your area soon! Check my events page for full details and get your tickets now. Alright, on with the show!"

Leaning forward dramatically, Gloria rested one elbow on the desk. With the other hand she put on a pair of huge tortoiseshell glasses.

"We are going to get smart and sassy for a moment. Because my friend Raffaella has worked her usual magic and conjured the most Glorious names for this line of nail colors." Gloria laughed her signature smoky chuckle. "These are delightful names that are just perfect for those of us who care about the impressions we make. We who know that anyone who doesn't do everything possible to enhance their presence is living a life of sad abnegation."

She held up a finger. "Let's consider that for a moment. As you know, I've made it my life's work to help anyone who wants help to improve their appearance. I've even worked with some who let themselves get to a state that can scarcely be called human. Imagine, misguided ladies who once went out in the morning without a full makeup, or who failed to update their hair color with the seasons. Some," Gloria shuddered, "were even letting their hair go gray." She wagged a finger. "You know who you are." She's turned on the full wattage of her smile. "And how glad you are that you are no longer behaving that way."

Settling back into her designer desk chair, Gloria put a serious look on her face. "I've enjoyed hearing your effusive thanks for my teaching you the true value of beauty and fashion. Sadly, there are still many, many, far too many, women in the world who refuse to pay attention to their appearance. There is nothing I can do for those creatures. We just have to leave them to their sorry fate. It's not up to us to waste our precious time trying to help those who won't be helped. But if you know someone who is willing to do what needs to be done, then by all means, send them to my channel."

She leaned forward again, and put delight into her voice once more.

"Now back to the product of the moment. What I find most appealing about the names Raffi has given these colors is the lack of actual descriptive words. As you know, I love a clever play on words that tells you everything you need to know about a hue. And these names do exactly that."

Gloria pointed her finger again and gave it a little professorial shake. "Listen now, here are the color names." Modulating her voice, she drew each word into a low, sleek, cultured sentence of its own. "Dubai. Yen. Booty. Krugerrand. Self-Made. Ruble. Oligarch. Night Trader." She paused. "Aren't those delightful? So literate and witty. Did you truly take in that last one? Night Trader. That is my favorite. Just soooo exquisitely cheeky."

Putting a quizzical look on her face, Gloria changed to a wondering tone. "You know, I'm beginning to suspect my pal Raffi has somehow resurrected Oscar Wilde to lead her branding team. Which means, of course, we'll have to keep an eye on her skin care line. Every cosmetics company has their age-defying products. But with these, I'm wondering – has Raffi leapt all the way to death-defying?" Gloria laughed uproariously at her joke.

"Alright now, thank you for putting up with my gushing over this world-class display of wordsmithery. I know you want to see the goods. So, here are the actual colors." Taking off the glasses, Gloria turned and with a flourish, held up a long, gold ceramic tray, tipping it so that it aligned with the angles of the silk draperies behind her to perfectly frame her face.

"Aren't these marvelous? Look at these shades. This is Dubai – which of course, would be sand. But not just any sand. This sand is composed of Carrara marble and pearls. Here's Yen – with its layered meanings of desire and wealth. A stratified pink made of cherry petals marinated in champagne. Mmm. And Booty," she laughed. "That's the name of this spicy ginger peach. It looks like summer sun glinting off your beautiful backside, no matter what shade that is, am I right? And who could mistake this for anything but Krugerrand – the sexiest, sexy, deep rose gold."Gloria tilted the tray to highlight the remaining four bottles. "Now, let's take a good look at the deeper side of this stunning palette. Oh, ladies, have you ever seen anything so desirable? This smoky, bourbon-and-tobacco-kissed red is called Self-Made." Next she held up a bright, blood red. "Oligarch." Putting the bottle back, she wagged a finger at the camera. "You knew that though, because that shade of red is just so naughty. Here's Ruble, what else, rubies and amber." She kissed the bottle. "Like a stolen kiss in the shadows of St. Basil's Cathedral. Which I recommend, by the way. See episode 753 for the story of my shoot in Red Square last year. I felt like a spy the whole time." She laughed and put the bottle down, paused and looked pointedly into the camera before picking up the last bottle.

"And finally, my darlings, this is Night Trader." Gloria held the bottle next to her heart. "Dark, dark, chocolate, kirsch, cherries and burgundy. Mmm, I want to eat it. Which means, I have an announcement for all my baking mavens. A recipe contest! Concoct your best dessert called Night Trader Dark, Dark, Chocolate, Kirsch, Cherry and Burgundy blank – cake, pie, cookies, mousse, the sky is the limit. The night sky." She laughed again.

"Send your recipe, along with a photo of you serving it while wearing this scrumptious color. Raffaella and I will bake your treat and choose the winner based on how good it tastes, how well it matches the polish, and also how clever and sexy your photo is. So do your very best on that photo." She turned, presented a sly side eye to the camera and dropped her voice. "Though we do want to keep it to an R rating, my dears. Let's not get the show banned for pornographic content."

"So there you have Raffi's latest coup. Rich, elegant, yet not conservative at all. These colors are not afraid to declare how much they are worth. And these bottles," she picked up one of the small sculpted vessels by its clear Lucite top. "Raffi is a marvel with the packaging, too, of course. And, as is my custom, I've arranged with Tiffany to come up with some very spectacular packaging of my own. I have a limited edition of ten of these sets for the most discerning of my fans."

"This Glorious package features all eight of Raffaela's shades, in this stunning Tiffany tray, for four hundred ninety dollars. Now we all know how hard it is to walk out of a Tiffany store for that little, and since the colors retail for fifty dollars each, that is just an incredible, incredible offer for my viewers only. Now aren't you glad you tuned in to this episode?"

She put the tray down on the desktop.

"One last thing – if one of you Glorious bakers makes Night Trader, Dark, Dark, Chocolate, Kirsch, Cherry and Burgundy cookie mousse cheesecake, that will win the Jump the Shark award and a bottle of Raffaella Revello Shark Tooth Skin Polish. It's the exfoliant I use to keep my complexion flawlessly smooth. It's got teeth." Gloria showed her own.

"Because when it comes to beauty, and to all of life honestly, prisoners are entirely too much trouble."

CHAPTER 1

On her way to the back door, Iris Winterbek picked up the phone and dialed her friend Emily. While the phone rang, she stepped into her plastic grocery bags and tied the handles around her ankles.

"Are you ready?" she asked when Emily answered. "I'll be there in twenty minutes."

"What's taking you so long? I've been ready for half an hour. I need a coffee right away. I've got my Senior Sneakers membership card. It gets me discounts on food at the casino restaurants." Emily reached out to a picture of a man in a pilot's uniform, laid it down on its face and gave it a gentle pat. "Drinks, too."

"I said I'd be there at eight," Iris said, as her Cocker Spaniel dashed out onto the lawn, barking joyously. "I just have to go out and pick up Rosie's poop and then I'm leaving."

"Gah. Whatever. Just get a move on. I'm up for this."

"Are you ready Amanda?" asked Iris, when the third member of their party picked up her phone.

"I'm working on it," Amanda said, breathing heavily. "I woke up all ready to go play at the casino with you and Emily, but my asthma is acting up. I've showered, dressed, and watered the garden, and now I'm ready for my morning nap." She took a deep breath and scooted her butt forward in preparation for rising. "First I have to get up out of this chair. I don't know what Ludwig was thinking when he came up with this Barcelona design. The seat seems to get lower every day. And no arms."

"You can do it," said Iris. "I'll see you in a few minutes."

After cleaning up the grass, putting Rosie in her kennel with her treat, and leaving a note for the dog sitter who would arrive that evening, Iris checked to make sure she had her key, then she opened the front door.

Something hit her in the forehead.

"OW!" Blinking, Iris reeled back and put a hand to her head.

"My god, Iris, that was stupid. You put your head right in the way of my knuckles."

"Mona?" The voice sounded like her sister. Iris was confused. "Why did you punch me in the face?"

"I did not punch you, I was simply knocking on your door," said Mona. "It's a common practice." She lowered her raised hand. The other hand, Iris now saw, gripped the handle of a rolling suitcase.

"Well, your aim has not improved since you threw that baseball through the windscreen of Dad's DeSoto." Iris rubbed her bruised brow. "What are you doing here?" Over Mona's shoulder she saw a bright yellow car turn the corner and speed away. Hell's bells. How was she going to get rid of this irritating intrusion if there was no cab to hustle Mona into?

"I came to see you."

"Really?" Iris found her mouth hanging open and closed it. "All the way from Idaho? Don't you have a nail salon or hairdresser appointment today?"

"No." Mona looked so bereft about this fact that Iris nearly burst out laughing.

"I have to talk to you," her sister continued.

Iris waved a hand. "Whatever it is, you should have called to tell me. I'm heading out the door for a day at the casino with my friends."

"It is too important to talk about over the phone."

Iris peered up at her sister's heavily made-up face. There was an earnest look under the layers of foundation and powder that she'd never seen there before.

"Well, come along then." Whatever was going on with Mona, they'd have to get to it later. She took out her keys, turned, and locked the door. "Tonight is Ladies' Night. We're staying over. So it's good you've got your suitcase. Come on. I'm late to pick up Amanda and Emily."

"Ladies' Night?" Mona perked up. "That means there will be men there, too. Ladies' Night is all about getting the men to come in. I need to use your bathroom to redo my makeup." She patted the side of her head and ran a hand over her hair. "I feel rather travel worn."

Iris rolled her eyes. "You can use my visor mirror to check your face." She gave Mona a gentle push toward the driveway, and the two of them wrestled Mona's huge suitcase into the trunk.

"Come on now, get in, hop to it." Iris started the car and put the pedal to the metal.

Emily's bright white house shone spic and span, as usual. The regimentally clipped hedges looked newly shorn. Emily shot out the front door, dressed in her customary trail-running shoes, walking shorts, and a t-shirt that said Sarcasm Loading, Please

Wait. A visor, vest, sunglasses, and a small duffel bag completed her ensemble. She yanked the back door open, said, "Iris, you're late," marched into a sitting position, and pointed to Mona. "Who is this?"

"This is my sister, Mona, from Coeur d'Alene," Iris said, as she carefully turned her stiff neck in preparation for backing out of the driveway. "She dropped in this morning, so I brought her along. Mona, this is my friend Emily from water aerobics."

"HelloMonaI'mEmilyHarriman."

"Hello Emily," said Mona. "I love your shirt."

"Thank you," said Emily. "It's from my spring collection."

Mona's painted-on eyebrows raised one-quarter inch. Iris smiled to herself. For Mona, who never let expression mar her visage, moving a facial feature that far was the equivalent of signaling the onset of a heart attack.

At Amanda's house, Iris turned off the car and made her way to the bright orange front door along a path barely visible through a riot of colorful flowers and foliage. Stepping over several soggy newspapers and a pair of tennis shoes, she picked up a rake that had fallen across the walk and propped it in the corner of the porch.

"Morning Amanda," said Iris when her friend answered her knock. Amanda was still wearing her slippers. "Why aren't you ready?"

"I'm ready. Just give me a second to get my shoes on."

Iris stepped into the foyer. "Can I help with anything?"

"No, thanks. They're here somewhere," Amanda said, wandering into the living room.

Amanda's house was like a gallery. Iris loved to look at the art. She'd been friends with people who were household names. A Warhol hung over her white leather couch. The dining table and chairs were hand carved, and in the center of the table sat one simple, rough, and slightly misshapen bowl that never failed to fascinate her. Amanda said it was by a Japanese master, but it looked like something Amy did in kindergarten. Except that it was somehow thrilling to look at.

Five minutes later, Iris hustled Amanda out the door, then waited while she checked all the locks.

Emily accosted Iris as soon as she got back in the car. "Iris, your sister says she didn't know you went to Europe. Why wouldn't you tell your family you were going to Europe?"

Iris shrugged into her seat belt. "She wouldn't have listened anyway." Iris had learned decades ago that if it wasn't about Mona, Mona wasn't interested.

Thankful that at least they were headed the opposite direction of morning rush hour traffic, Iris was finally aiming the car at the freeway on-ramp a block distant when suddenly, Mona grabbed her arm.

"What?" she yelped, startled by the unexpected contact.

"Turn in here Iris. I have to get some money. Those casino ATMs will rob you blind."

"Come on, tell us about your trip, Iris," said Emily. "Amy told me you were used as a mule."

Iris turned in to the bank driveway, then squeaked as the car jounced over a speed hump. "My lord, where did that come from?"

"She's busy driving," said Amanda. "Give her a moment. What kind of car is this Iris? I like this upholstery, it's really soft."

"Take it easy on the bumps, Iris. My shoulder is just healing up from that bicycle accident."

"We visited Amsterdam, London, Cornwall, Scotland and Ireland, and we had a great time. Amy is a wonderful travel planner. She plans trips all the time, of course, for her job. She found us the most beautiful hotel room in Dublin."

"The man who lives next door to me is Irish. He has measles," said Amanda. "How weird is that for an adult to have measles?"

"I saw a story about that on 60 Minutes. It can be quite debilitating for older adults," said Mona as she got out. The others watched her straighten her stiff back and slowly walk to the cash machine.

"You told me you're the baby of the family," said Emily. "So she must be your big sister, right?"

"That's right. She's two years older than me. So . . . my god, she's just turned eighty. That seems so old."

"She looks reasonably healthy for her age. And she looks like you. The same straight posture, the same wavy hair."

"Just taller and more sophisticated. Right, Mona?" Iris said as her sister opened the door.

"If you are asking if I am more sophisticated than you, I'd say that's obvious to anyone with eyes." Mona carefully settled herself back into her seat and smoothed her skirt over her thin knees.

"There's no excuse for getting any of those childhood diseases," said Emily. "All you have to do is eat leafy greens every day. Also yogurt, that really helps."

Amanda and Iris let a silence fall after Emily's pronouncement. Both of them were wise enough to avoid getting into a debate this early in the day.

"Speaking of illness," said Iris, as she pulled back out onto the street. "In Edinburgh we led a tour of an underground street that was walled up during the plague. It was really exciting."

"Ewww!" Amanda covered her mouth with both hands.

"What do you mean, led?" said Emily.

"Oh my god, Iris. How could you?" Mona leaned away from her sister as if she were about to start vomiting black blood. "That daughter of yours always has been irresponsible. And you're just weak to go along with her shenanigans. She would never convince me to enter such a place, I can tell you. The germs and the filth . . . I'm just too sensitive. I'd get ill on the spot."

Iris wanted to shout – "You make me ill on this spot!" – but she held her tongue, as usual. She did glare at her sister. Which had no effect. Mona stared straight ahead, her look unconcerned.

Silence descended again. Which made Iris uncomfortable. They were supposed to be having fun and here Mona was, screwing up everything. She'd much rather have had Sam Chandler's mom, Paula, join them.

Iris had met Sam on the plane to Amsterdam. Though their relationship had started rockily, they'd become friends and they'd got into all kinds of adventures together when she joined in with Sam's hobby of play-acting scenes from books. She'd called Sam's mother just after she and Amy got home from Europe and had a wonderful time telling her all about their escapades with her son.

"My son is a caution," Mrs. Chandler had said, with a laugh that reminded Iris of Sam. "He made me play a nun once in one of his little skits. I was so embarrassed, but we had a great time." She went on to describe how, curious about what a confessional looked like, she'd wound up stuck inside the ancient wooden box and Sam hadn't noticed she was missing until she wasn't there to say her lines. The rest of the players had searched for her. They'd finally had to hire a carpenter to remove the door and get her out. Too bad Iris hadn't thought to invite her along on this trip. She'd be a lot more fun than Mona.

"By the way," Iris said, looking at Emily and Amanda in the rearview mirror. "Amy and I met a young man on the plane – the one who set up the underground tour – and I've talked with his mother. I think she'd be a great addition to our group. Maybe we can all get together for tea next week. I think you'd like . . ."

"Iris. Watch where you're going. You're going to hit that rock wall."

Mona's bark brought her back to what she was doing. She'd taken her eyes off the road just as she was turning in at the Blackfish Casino entrance. She yanked the little car back into the lane just in time.

"Not that this tin can would do any damage," said Mona.

"Well, that wall would give the car a pain," said Emily. "So I'd suggest paying attention to what you're doing Iris."

"Speaking of paying attention," said Amanda, "I've set a one-hundred-dollar gambling limit for myself today. I'm not going to be a victim again."

"Hah! That reminds me, Iris, I want to know how you were a victim in Europe. Tell us about this mule incident," said Emily as Iris pulled up to valet parking.

"Mule incident? What is a mule incident?" said Mona.

"I don't know," said Emily. "Something happened in Amsterdam. Amy said Iris was horribly taken advantage of by a terrible man. He abused her, treated her abominably."

Amanda thrust her arm forward between the seats. They all turned to look in the direction she was pointing.

CHAPTER 2

In the center of the portico, a woman in a pale pink suit, her blond hair piled high in an elegant up do, was repeatedly slapping a young valet across the face.

The boy staggered back across the paving tiles and, with a yelp, tripped backward into the bed of red ornamental grass and blue Russian sage that lined the arcing drive. As he fell, he narrowly missed braining himself on a granite boulder.

The door of a sleek, gold luxury car stood open behind the woman. Still shrieking at the boy, she stiletto-stalked back to the vehicle and pulled something out from under the windshield wiper, waved it at him, crumpled it, and tossed it on the ground. Iris' car rolled to a halt as the friends sat there stunned, watching this display.

"Oh, look," said Emily, "an unkindness of socialites. It only takes one."

"She littered." said Amanda beginning to wheeze. "She shouldn't litter. A woman of her stature must set a good example for the younger generation."

"That is one beautiful suit," said Mona. "Chanel. I've always wanted a Chanel suit."

"I love her bag," said Amanda. She looked down at the ramshackle tapestry tote perched on her knees. "I need a new bag." She looked up again. "Why would such a lovely woman be so horrible to that kid?" She pulled out her inhaler and took a long draw.

"Yeah, I wonder what the young hooligan did," said Emily, eyes narrowed. "It must be his fault, right?"

"I don't care what he did, nothing is worthy of that kind of behavior," Iris said. "But I faced worse than her in Ireland. I'll take care of this."

Iris got out of the car, puffed herself up, and with a return of the glow of accomplishment she'd felt while taking down bad guys at the Giant's Causeway on the north coast of Ireland, marched over to confront the terrible woman. "See here . . ." she began. Out of the corner of her eye she saw Emily sprint around the car, plow into the garden and extend a hand to the victim.

The woman gave Iris the literal back of her hand, brushing her aside like a gnat. "Get out of my way, Grandma," she said without even looking at Iris. "Go put your pension into my slot machines where it belongs."

"Your slot machines?" said Iris, blood boiling.

The woman ignored her and strode toward the entrance, flinging one last command over her shoulder. "Don't you dare touch that vehicle again, you idiot."

"Are you calling me an idiot?" Iris was aghast.

"Ma'am you can't just leave . . ." said the valet, stepping toward the car door the woman had left open. Before he could reach it, the door shut and the car started down the drive. The boy stood stunned for a moment, then pulled his arm from Emily's grasp and ran after the car.

"Wait," he called. "Stop. What about my tip?"

The friends stood stupefied as the car drove away by itself. Emily recovered first.

"That must be a self-driving Tesla! I didn't know they were available yet. How exciting to see one in real life."

After the Tesla and the valet disappeared around the bend, the friends regrouped around Iris.

"Iris, I don't know how you do it," Amanda said, breathing hard.

"Do what?" said Iris. She was still gazing after the retreating woman, peeved at herself for not knocking her on her backside while she had the chance. She could have. If ony she'd remembered to use her one martial arts move. Drat her slow wits. She needed to sharpen up if she was going to have any luck today.

"Drive with those bags on your feet. Aren't they slippery?" Everyone looked down.

"Well, well," said Emily.

Mona rolled her eyes heavenward. Iris felt her face get very red as she stooped and clawed the plastic bags loose from her feet, exposing a pair of battered, matted, and no longer white, fuzzy slippers.

"Oh, no," she felt like crying. "I left my shoes on the front porch. Mona, why didn't you tell me I was still wearing these?"

"I didn't notice. But now that you mention it, I should have assumed there would be something I'd need to improve about your outfit. I've had to do it all your life. So the fact that you've got garbage bags tied on your feet is obviously my bad."

The young valet trudged up the drive, red-faced, and asked if he could help them.

"Yes, please," said Iris. "Could you have our suitcases brought in? We have rooms reserved. We're here for Ladies' Night."

"We have to stay over because none of us likes to drive after dark," said Amanda.

"And the free drinks don't start until eight o'clock," said Emily.

The valet smiled and asked Iris to open the trunk.

"We need you to park the car, too," said Emily.

"No," said Iris. "First we have to use it to go back home to get my shoes."

"What?" said Mona. "We can't leave, we just got here."

"Does anyone have any spare shoes?"

"Not that would fit those tiny stubs you call feet," said Emily. "I wear an eight."

"Me too," said Mona.

"I didn't bring any others," said Amanda.

"There's an outlet mall just across the parking lot," said the valet.

Iris looked where he was pointing. "That's right. Wonderful. I'll get some new shoes there, then we won't lose so much gambling time. Back in the car girls."

"Are you kidding?" said Emily. "I haven't had my coffee yet. I hate shopping. I sure can't face an outlet mall without caffeine. We have to have coffee first. And I have to take a picture of all of us." She pulled out her phone and handed it to the valet. "Gather round here."

"But my shoes . . ."

"Iris, just get in here, Emily needs her coffee, so let's get this over with," said Mona.

"There's an espresso place just inside the lobby there," the valet said, handing back the phone and pointing toward the main door.

"I can't go in there. I haven't got any shoes." The others looked at Iris' feet again.

"You'll be fine, Iris," said Amanda. "No one will see your feet. They'll be under the table."

Emily tipped the valet, asked him to leave the car where it was for half an hour, and the group started inside.

"Whatever," said Iris, dragging along after her friends, trying to hide her slippers by walking in the shadows of the potted palms.

"I hope we don't run into that bitch in there," said Mona, looking toward the casino entrance. Iris' attention snapped toward her sister. She frowned. They say it takes one to know one, she thought. But criticizing entitled, disrespectful people was the last thing Iris expected from an entitled, disrespectful person.

"This is just so beautiful," said Amanda, gazing up at the cedar and driftwood ceiling. Iris followed her gaze. It was nice, then she looked down again and noticed that the floor looked like polished sand.

"There are a few too many mirrors for my taste," said Emily.

"I rather like the effect," said Mona, smiling at herself and raising a hand to smooth her hair.

A cluster of people in business attire stood in the lobby, talking softly. It sounded to Iris like they were cooing over a baby. Then she saw a flash of pink and realized that the navy blue and black suits were encircling the nasty woman who'd hit the valet. Through a slot between a woman wearing a black suit and towering heels, and a man in pinstriped charcoal, she glimpsed the blond woman's face, upturned, red-lipstick-fake-smiling into a cell phone. Selfies. Bah. She must be a celebrity, the way they kept fawning over her.

Iris turned away, trying to ignore the sickening sounds of adulation.

"Who is that?" Amanda voiced the question on Iris' mind.

"No one I know," said Mona, as if that meant the woman was no one at all.

A chef, carrying an ornate and gleaming cake, swept between Iris and the desk. She nearly crashed into him.

"Iris, for heaven's sake. Pay attention to where you're going," said Mona, grabbing Iris' arm and yanking her out of the way.

They watched as the circle opened to admit the chef. The oohs and ahhs turned from the woman to the cake, and one of the men waved a flourishing hand toward it.

"On behalf of Blackfish Hotel management, I'm honored to present you with the *piece de resistance* from our new dessert menu – the Goldwater Cake. We'll serve it to your fans at the brunch."

My god, thought Iris, this mean person was being feted by the casino executives. Was she some kind of hero? Maybe she was a high roller. She certainly looked the part.

"She must have hit a jackpot," said Emily. "They'll be treating me like that later after my big win."

"New money would explain her abysmal behavior, I suppose," said Amanda. "They say it can change a person." She sounded dubious, though, and immediately took another hit from her inhaler.

"You're all just jealous," said Mona. "She looks perfectly lovely, and all these folks seem to like her. Just because one incompetent valet pissed her off doesn't mean she's not a wonderful person."

Iris glared at her sister, walked to the check-in desk, tucked her slippered feet under the edge of the counter and gave the clerk their names. Leaning forward as far as the high counter would allow, she whispered to the desk clerk.

"Excuse me, who is that woman?"

The clerk smiled in what Iris thought was an overly sweet way. "That is Gloria Trammel? You probably recognize her from the news? She's very prominent in the Northwest social scene. No? Her channel is very exciting? She's a lifestyle, fashion and beauty vlogger?"

"A what?" said Iris.

"She does beauty videos?" asked Mona, turning to look at the woman in pink with renewed interest. "I watch all the best beauty and fashion channels, but I don't recognize her. She must not have broken out of the Seattle market yet."

Iris smiled at the blinking clerk apologetically. Once again her incorrigible sister had managed to put someone down with hardly any effort.

"You mean YouTube videos?" said Emily. "I watch the birding channels. But I've never bothered with that beauty stuff."

"Clearly," said Mona.

"I subscribe to art channels," said Amanda. "The Guggenheim is my favorite, but the MOMA videos are great, too."

"Museum videos?" said Iris. "Why not just go to the museum?"

"I can't get to every show," said Amanda. "Videos let me keep up on things."

"I don't get it," said Iris. "I don't have any interest in watching videos of people showing off clothes or art."

"You'd enjoy the dog channels, Iris," said Mona. "Obsessed as you are with that little mongrel of yours."

"She's not a mongrel. She's a purebred Cocker Spaniel." Iris stopped. "Wait. I have watched videos of the Westminster Dog Show. Is that what you mean?"

The clerk broke in. "Besides her YouTube channel, Gloria is also Steve Trammel's wife." She smiled at them. Their faces must have let her know they had no idea what she was talking about. "The director of the state gaming commission? He oversees all the casinos in the state? They stay here often. We're featured in her videos many times. The spa especially. Very nice people." The clerk nodded too many times.

"Oh, really?" said Emily.

"You should ask the valet how nice she is," said Mona. Iris couldn't help staring at her sister. Her opinions seemed to be veering all over the place.

Check-in done, Iris and Emily arranged for their bags to be sent to the correct rooms. Then Iris began passing the key cards out. Emily and Amanda tucked their key cards into purses and pockets and started toward the coffee shop. Mona was standing in the entrance beside a tall young man in a business suit. Iris watched as her crazy sister smoothed her platinum blond hair, batted her eyelashes and lightly touched the fellow's woolen sleeve. Sighing and dangling her purse beside her in an effort to hide her feet from the perfectly fashionable group, Iris swept in. "Excuse us, we have an appointment," she said to the man and pried Mona off him.

"Isn't he handsome Iris? He's just so attractive and well put together. I think that suit is Armani."

"He's also sixty-five years younger than you." Iris could not help snapping at her ridiculous sister. "You need to get a grip, Mona. His grandparents are younger than you."

Mona obviously didn't hear her, she was busy looking over her shoulder at the kid and giving him a finger wiggle wave. Iris just sighed.

***

At the outlet mall, Amanda, Emily, and Mona trailed after Iris from store to store as she searched for just the right pair of shoes. They even went into the Puma sports store because she saw some white sneakers in the window that might work. Iris thought Mona would strain her eyeball muscles, so hard did she roll her eyes at that suggestion.

They were passing the door of the Ann Taylor outlet when Amanda suddenly said, "Look, Handbag Warehouse. I could get a new knitting bag there."

Sure enough, two doors down was a store that carried only handbags, purses and wallets. Emily let the door fall shut. It smashed into Mona, who wobbled and broke out into a short stream of cursing.

"Some of us want to get something other than shoes. I'm going to look at those scarves," she said, pushing the door open again. "We'll go in here for a moment, then head over to the handbag place."

"But we have to get Iris to another shoe store," said Emily, who was displaying signs of impatience.

"I don't know why you have to hustle us around like this," said Amanda slowly revolving a jewelry display in search of a new pair of earrings. "My heart is pounding from the pace. Slow down and take your time, Emily."

"If I stand too long my back starts to hurt," said Emily crossly. "I like to keep moving."

"Maybe it hurts because you move too much," said Amanda. "You only have so much energy. You don't want to use it up too soon."

"Hah," said Emily, "so you're one of those. No wonder you like to sit around so much. The opposite is true – movement makes energy. I say, use it or lose it."

CHAPTER 3

Emily stood grumbling and tapping her foot for a few minutes, while the others shopped. Finally they moved on to the handbag store and while Emily grumbled some more, Amanda began looking at old-fashioned tapestry totes similar to her current one. They reminded Iris of carpetbags. She'd always hated those things.

"Look, Amanda. Over there on the wall." Iris pointed to a display of pale pastel leather totes similar to the one the woman in pink had been carrying. Amanda lit up.

"Ohhh! Those are perfect," said Amanda, dropping the carpetbag and sailing across the store. She grasped a pale yellow bag and ran her hands over it. She looked up and held the bag open for the gang to see inside, then hugged the creamy yellow leather to her bosom. "This is perfect for my knitting. Plus, it reminds me of butter."

Emily had taken down a blue-tinted version. "Look at all the pockets. I think this one is about the right size for my birding binoculars." She held the purse down near her sandals. "Though I think it's just too pale, I'll get it dirty out in the woods."

"Good call, it's basically white," said Mona, then she looked thoughtful. "I think that peach tone would go with the scarf I just bought." She pushed Emily aside and peered up at the peach model. "Excuse me," she called across the store.

A clerk looked up. "Yes ma'am?" She trotted toward them. "What can I help you with?"

"I need you to get this peach bag down for me."

"Oh, for heaven's sake, Mona," said Iris. "I can get that down and I'm four inches shorter than you. And you have heels on."

"Let her earn her pay," said Mona.

"You should at least say please," Iris said, looking apologetically at her two friends who were staring at Mona as she inspected the bag, criticizing its stitching to the clerk.

"Is this Prada?"

"It's similar," said the clerk, blushing a little.

"Similar?" said Mona, down her nose.

"Oh, look," Iris said, to distract everyone from her uncouth sister. "It comes in this lavender tint, too. I really like that yellow, Amanda, but as you know, lavender is my color."

"You need to clean your glasses," said Emily. "That's pink."

"It's clearly lavender," said Iris. "And look, with the adjustable strap, I can wear it cross body, the way I like." She lengthened the strap, put it over her head and looked in the mirror. It did look nice. She and Amanda went to the counter with their purchases. Emily, who'd decided she didn't need a purse after all, trailed along, still grousing about wasting time.

After sufficiently browbeating the help, Mona opted to buy the peach tote and they all trooped out of the store very pleased with themselves for finding the best purse on the planet.

With the friends distracted by their purchases, Iris was finally able to focus on finding a decent pair of comfortable shoes without their conflicting advice.

Back in the car, Amanda immediately began switching her knitting and other belongings from her old battered tote to the new yellow one. Iris, watching her in the rearview mirror, thought it made a big improvement to her friend's ensemble.

"Hey, watch where you're waving those knitting needles." Emily slapped a hand over her arm. "Those are deadly weapons. I think you drew blood." Emily rolled up the sleeve of her t-shirt. Sure enough, there was a red scratch, but it wasn't bleeding.

"Oh, no. I'm so sorry, Emily." Amanda's face was white. "There are usually little rubber stoppers on the tips. I must have lost one." She rummaged in her old bag. Iris worried she'd start wheezing again. She was going to use up her inhaler before lunch at the rate she was going. Time for a change of subject.

"I don't know, Amanda . . . While I really like the lavender tint of my purse, I think I might have to fight you for that yellow one. It's so beautiful."

"Oh, brother," said Emily. "Don't worry that I'll steal your handbag, Mona. I've never liked peach."

"They're all so pale, it's like they're just white seen in different light," said Amanda. "White can be really tricky. There are so many shades . . . in nature, in paints. I have this problem with white yarn all the time. I make something that I think has a warm cast, then I go outside and someone compliments me on my pretty blue sweater. What are you doing with all those latex gloves?"

Emily had been cleaning out the pockets of her vest. She stopped what she was doing and looked up. "They're for handling dead birds." She pulled out a roll of plastic bags. "When I find one I put it in a bag. The lab wants the carcasses for testing so they can find out what killed them."

"You're not going to pull out a dead bird next, are you?" Iris said, steering the car back on the road again. "No dead bodies in my car!" She glanced at Mona, expecting her to have some choice comment about uncleanliness. Her sister appeared not to have heard and was meticulously tucking her can of hair spray into the proper pocket of her new, sherbet-colored bag. Then she leaned back in her seat and closed her eyes, a look on her face that Iris couldn't put her finger on. Something was wrong.

"Mona, when you're done, would you please shift my stuff to my new bag, too? I don't want to carry my old scuffed purse when you both look so nice."

Begrudgingly, Mona opened her eyes and took Iris' new purse out of the store bag. "I can't break this plastic doohickey. You should have had the tag removed at the checkout like I did. You never think ahead, Iris."

"Here, I have scissors," said Amanda and Emily in unison. They both held up small pairs. Mona took Amanda's, cut the plastic strip, removed the tag, and handed them back over the seat. Then she opened Iris' old gray purse and started moving things. Iris ground her teeth as her wallet and glasses case were tossed in. Mona wasn't nearly as careful with Iris' things as she was with her own. It made her cross to watch. She really needed a new wallet, she should have looked for . . .

"Why do you have all these plastic grocery bags wadded up in here? Are you expecting to encounter dead things, too, or do you need to cover your new shoes? Oh. Spare underwear, Iris?"

Iris was beginning to regret having her sister do this job. Now Mona knew more than was good for her.

Mona held up a blue cylinder. "What's this?"

"Oh, that's the handiest little gadget. Amy gave it to me when we were in Ireland. Pull on the end."

Mona did as instructed. "It telescopes out . . ."

"Isn't that cool? It's a telescoping walking stick. Very handy. I also use it to knock things off high shelves."

Mona sighed and collapsed the stick. "Whatever." She tossed it into the bag. "Alright ladies," said Mona, slapping Iris' bag closed. As they pulled up to valet parking again she took a deep breath. "I'm ready to go win my jackpot now." She pulled down the visor, checked her makeup, and applied a fresh coat of lipstick. Then she draped the new scarf around her neck. "Let's do this."

Finally, thought Iris giddily. Caffeinated, comfy in her new shoes, and with a stunning new tote on her arm, she let herself be drawn toward the music of the slots. Wafted forward on a cloud of hope and excitement, she approached her destiny.

"I can't face those bells and flashing lights on an empty stomach," said Amanda. "I need to get breakfast."

"You had a cinnamon roll when we had coffee," said Emily, "not much more than half an hour ago."

"That wasn't breakfast though," said Amanda. "That was just a treat. I need protein."

"Protein is always a good idea," said Mona, sounding only slightly sarcastic.

"I really want to get in there," Iris said. All these delays. She could feel that hundred-dollar bill threatening to ignite her wallet. But Mona did look wan. It would be no fun if she collapsed from low blood sugar.

Amanda stopped in front of the Birch Bark Cafe. "Just a quick bite."

"Fine," said Iris, trying not to grumble.

Once they had ordered, Emily turned to Iris. "Now, the mule story. Go."

"Oh, Emily. I'm so embarrassed." A giggle escaped. "I'm afraid I did let myself be taken advantage of." But she was also kind of proud. She'd been in and out of some frightening situations. At the time she'd been afraid she was going to die. In hindsight, it was all quite thrilling.

Amanda nodded, smiling and encouraging. Emily turned toward her on the seat, drumming her fingernails on the table. Mona closed her eyes, nostrils flared. It looked like no one really wanted to hear all the exciting things that happened.

"It all started at breakfast one morning, in our hotel in Amsterdam. It was a lovely old Amsterdam house on a canal. Really charming. Anyway, you know that the hotels there are mostly bed and breakfast, everyone gets together in the morning . . ."

"We know," said Mona.

Iris chose to ignore the interruption. "Amy was being bossy about something, I forget what, and then she left and I remember, I was a little irritated with her."

"Iris, come on." Emily stopped the drumming and smacked her hand on the table, "your relationship with your daughter is not what we want to hear about"

Iris glared at her. "Well then I'll just cut to the chase. A man gave me a gift. Okay? Happy now?"

"Why would you take a gift from a strange man, Iris?" Amanda was about to start hitting the inhaler again, Iris could tell.

"He was nice to me and it was lovely. Beautifully wrapped. It was in paper that looked like Delft, the blue and . . ."

"Iris!" Mona barked and Iris jumped. People at neighboring tables turned their way.

"We just want the facts about what happened, dear," said Emily. "You can leave out the description of the paper. It's not important."

"I think it's important," Iris retorted. "If the package hadn't been pretty I wouldn't have taken it. Would you take a banged up package wrapped in brown paper?"

"Was it small?" asked Amanda. "Good things come in small packages."

"It was small, but it wasn't good. That's a misconception. It was a box of incense . . ."

"What? You hate incense," said Mona. "Why did you take it?"

"Because it was pretty and given to me by a nice man." Iris found herself almost shouting and lowered her voice. "I just told you it was wrapped up. I couldn't smell it."

"What did you do with it?" Mona asked.

"I put it in my purse and forgot about it." Iris smiled at the memory.

"And just carried it across a border? You took a mysterious package through customs?" Mona's eyebrows were creeping slightly upward.

"Haven't you heard all the warnings?" Amanda asked.

Iris sat up and looked around. "What warnings?"

"The airport warnings about not letting anyone put anything in your bag." Mona had that tone in her voice again.

"We weren't at the airport," said Iris, anger at her sister returning. "We were in a restaurant. Do you want to hear the story or not?"

Emily dabbed her lips with her napkin and grasped Mona's wrist across the table. "Mona, we're going to have to let her tell the story her way."

"Thank you, Emily." Iris smoothed her ruffled hair. "I put the package in my purse. In London my bag was searched at customs. I think it was London. Anyway, they didn't find the package, or it wasn't anything they were interested in. They were more interested in the bottle with the blood on it."

"Blood!?" said Amanda.

"Criminy," said Mona.

"How exhilarating," said Emily. "Amy never mentioned a bloody bottle."

Iris thought a moment. "At the time I thought it was jam. Anyway, they let us go and we left. Oh, and someone tried to steal my purse."

"Oh, no!" Amanda clutched her new bag.

"Then there was the car chase in Scotland. But we could never figure out what was happening until we got to the Giant's Causeway and some thugs kidnapped Amy."

"Kidnapped!?" said all three listeners in unison.

"Except they didn't."

"Hold on," said Emily.

"I thought there were going to be mules," said Amanda shaking her head. "I'm not sure I'm following this."

"How could you?" said Mona. She looked around for the waiter. "I think I'll order a vodka. Anyone else want one?"

Peevishly, Iris noticed that, other than dragging her fork around in the sauce, Mona hadn't touched her Eggs Benedict. The hollandaise was just sitting there congealing. She wouldn't drink the vodka, either. She was just pulling Iris' chain again, and finding one more way of putting her down in front of her friends. Her sister was so profoundly irritating.

"I'm tempted to join you," said Emily, "but it's way too early. Besides, my head is already spinning." She turned back to Iris.

"Iris, dear, I want to get one thing clear. Did you still have the package when you went across all those borders?"

"No."

Emily sat back and shook her head as if to clear it. "Then why did these things keep happen . . ."

Iris blew up. "Well no one knew that did they? And it wasn't until after the accident that Hal found me and . . ."

30

"Who's Hal?" said Emily.

"What accident?" said Amanda.

Iris clamped her mouth shut and folded her arms. Mona was sitting still with her eyes closed again, no expression on her face. That was even more irritating than if she'd been smirking at all the drama she'd caused.

Emily got up, jostling against Mona who jerked, as if waking. "I'm going to the casino. At this point I'd prefer to listen to all the jangling bells. And if I don't get out of here I'm going to end up ordering a double vodka, too early or not."

The other two followed her. As they went out the door, Iris, still sitting in the booth, trying to cool off, heard Amanda ask Emily, "Did I miss the bit about the mule?" There was nothing to do but laugh. She decided she was actually relieved not to have to tell any more of the story. It only got more complex.

CHAPTER 4

"I need to use the ladies' room," said Amanda as Iris caught up to the others. Emily looked at the ceiling, and Mona let go a few choice comments. But nothing could persuade Amanda to wait a while, and in the end they all trooped in after her.

As she pushed open the door of a stall, Iris heard Amanda gasp, then the sound of her inhaler again. She was certainly using her medication liberally.

Navigating a stream of noisy and heavily made-up young women coming in to check their lipstick, Iris headed out to wait for her friends in the lobby. She turned out of the lounge and into the narrow hall that wound around a couple of corners. There was a door at the end. This didn't look right. She didn't remember there being another door, but she pushed it open. A uniformed man was reaching up and running a cloth over some wires. There were a lot of other wires and cables in that room.

The man turned to look at her and seemed to be about to speak. Then he jumped aside, backing up against the wall of wiring. He was small, not much taller than Iris herself, slight, had a bushy mustache and wore a peaked cap like a police officer. His eyes were red rimmed.

"I'm sorry," said Iris. "I must have turned the wrong way." She smiled, backed out and closed the door. How strange, she thought as she made her way back down the hall past another wave of chattering women in expensive clothing.

"Where have you been?" Mona asked, as she came to the lobby and found the group waiting for her.

"I turned the wrong way up the hall. There was a strange young man hiding in an electrical room, crying. It was a little unnerving"

"I found a strange young man, too," said Amanda. "He was in the first stall I tried, putting on a fake mustache."

Mona snorted. "He probably identifies as female."

"Well, if that's the case, he's not comfortable with it yet. He turned beet red and slammed the door on my fingers."

This time, as she walked through the elegant foyer, Iris felt more human. She loved these shiny new loafers, and the pale lavender bag on her shoulder went well with her favorite blouse. She didn't fit in with the clusters of fashionable young women now thronging the space, but then she never had, even when she was much younger.

The woman in pink Chanel was gone and the reception clerks stared into their computer monitors. Down the hall behind them Iris saw other workers busy at desks, just like in any office. As she was turning away, a flash of pink appeared from around a corner and there was that awful woman again. She was leaning forward and . . . ack! Iris looked away quickly as the woman in pink kissed someone who was mostly hidden behind a pillar. Who would want to kiss that terrible person? Only another terrible person. That meant there were two terrible people in this place. She shuddered. The others were chatting noisily ahead of her and she trotted to catch up, putting the spectacle out of her mind and vowing to keep from looking down any more hallways.

With a contented sigh, Iris settled in behind a Blooming Lotus machine and watched the flowers bloom and the gems sparkle. This was so much more entertaining than years ago, when it was just mechanical pictures of cherries and oranges sliding by. That old style had its own sense of drama, but these were downright beautiful. She tucked her bill into the slot, watched it get sucked away into the void and proceeded to place her bet.

She played game after game, winning most of them. She'd just doubled her money again and was gleefully playing another bonus round when there was a tugging on her arm.

"Iris. Please, I have to get out of here for a while." Amanda was wheezing.

"Okay," Iris said, dismayed at having to leave a machine that was paying. But all morning she'd been worried that something was up with her friend's health. "Just a second. Sit down while I cash out."

Mona and Emily were standing at the end of the row. Mona was looking at the ceiling. Emily was tapping her foot.

"I just need some fresh air," Amanda said. "I usually only do one thing per day. I guess this is all just too much." Iris felt like she'd missed something. Nothing here was too much for her. Could Amanda still be dwelling on the altercation at the entrance? She followed her friends and her sister to the exit.

"I guess I'm ready for a break, too," said Emily, "we have been sitting too long. It's a beautiful morning. Let's hit the trail back there in the woods and stretch our legs."

Good lord, thought Iris, Emily was as bad as Amy. Her daughter was always wanting her to stretch her legs.

As they passed the elevators, Emily stopped and took out her key card.

"I'm gonna go up to the room and take off this vest so I don't get sweaty."

"Oh, for god's sake. We're not going to jog," said Mona. "Hurry up, I'm tired of standing around waiting for people. I don't have much time."

"Emily moves quickly," said Iris, puzzled by the statement. "We'll go ahead, Em. You can catch up." She turned to her sister. "She'll probably be back before we get to the door."

Sure enough, they'd only been outside the door for a moment when Emily rejoined them.

Mona looked down at Emily's feet and visibly recoiled. "I have never understood this penchant for wearing socks with sandals. If your feet are ugly, wear shoes."

They all looked down. Emily's blue woolen toes protruded from the front of her chunky sandals. "I like to be able to wiggle my toes," said Emily, demonstrating.

Iris was heartened to see that Emily was out of breath. Maybe she wouldn't push them to walk so fast.

"Girls," Emily said, sotto voce as they headed down the side walk. I just saw the strangest thing." She took a deep breath and gathered them into a cluster. "I was coming out of the room . . . It's quite nice, by the way. We have a view of the forest path. And the parking lot. And the loading dock. But I think we can look past those. You'll love the art, Amanda."

"Wonderful, but what did you see?" said Amanda, as breathless as Emily.

"Just as I was closing the door, the elevator opened. A waiter wheeled a cart out. He looked around, but I guess he didn't see me. There was a big vase of flowers between us, so maybe I was hidden behind them. Anyway, he lifted a corner of the tablecloth off the cart, looked around again, took a pistol out of his pocket and slid it underneath the cloth."

Amanda and Iris gasped. Mona narrowed her eyes – but not enough to risk a wrinkle.

"You're dreaming. Or," she wagged a finger in Emily's face, "you've been watching Oceans Eleven."

Emily visibly bristled. Iris thought maybe her friend was beginning to see the problem with having Mona along. "I am perfectly clearheaded and I haven't seen that movie in years. I know what I saw. And in fact, I have to note that this man was quite small, wore a peaked cap, and had a mustache. He disappeared into a room. I couldn't wait for the elevator. I ran down three flights of stairs to tell you."

Ran? Iris' heart sunk. "Let's walk a little slower," she said, modifying her pace for Amanda and hoping Emily would do the same.

"Do you suppose it was the same man?" asked Amanda.

"Which same man, the one Iris saw in the closet, or the one you saw in the toilet? Because it can't be both." Mona fell into step with Amanda.

Iris tried to bring them back to reality. "The important bit isn't who the man was, the important bit is what is he, or anybody for that matter, doing hiding a gun on a room service cart? Emily, could it have been something else? Maybe the bill? Those bill folder things are about the right size. They're sometimes black. It must have been the bill."

Emily stopped walking and turned a baleful gaze on her. "It was a gun."

"What do you propose we do about it?" asked Mona as they caught up to Emily. "Did you take a picture? Do you have evidence of what you saw? If you did, we could go to the desk and report him."

"No, I didn't get a picture, dang it."

"You're kidding," said Amanda. "You've been taking pictures of everything. How could you miss taking one of something so important?"

"I should have." Emily looked cross. "I will next time. I'll keep my eyes open and be ready. The rest of you, if you see one of those tiny, mustachioed men again, let me know and I'll snap his picture." She turned and started walking again and Iris, Amanda and Mona followed.

Amanda broke out laughing. "I just had a funny thought. We've seen a man putting on a fake mustache, a guy messing with some kind of wiring, and another hiding a gun. I feel like we're in one of those silly caper movies where the bad guys set up some elaborate plan that costs more money than the theft will net them."

The other three turned and stared at her. After a moment, her laughter subsided. "Oh," she said, and started wheezing again. "Maybe we are." She pulled another dose from her inhaler.

Emily turned and headed up the path. She had just rounded the bend in the path and disappeared into the trees with her binoculars trained on the branches, when Mona grabbed Iris' arm.

"Iris, slow up a little. We need to talk."

"So talk," said Iris, slowing a tiny bit.

Amanda walked on into the shade, fanning herself.

"Let's let them get ahead a bit. It's important, and I don't want any silly comments."

Iris stopped and put her hands on her hips. "Who are you calling silly? Are you talking about my friends?" It was one thing for Mona to criticize her, but her friends were off limits. After everything Mona had said already this morning, she felt ready to spit fire in defense of Emily and Amanda.

"You know you don't have to be here. I didn't invite you. You just showed up on my doorstep with your suitcase and your attitude. So if none of us are up to your standards, I suggest you leave." She dug in her bag and pulled out her phone. "I'll gladly call you a cab right now."

"Calm down, Iris. I didn't mean to offend anyone, but I thought you didn't much like these women. Emily cares only about birds and thinks you're frivolous. Earlier you were mad at Amanda with her messy house and her crazy knitting all over the place and that truly ugly old bag she was carrying. Yet you let her direct everything. First she needs a purse, then she needs food, then she needs the ladies' room, and now we're out here in the heat because she needs air. What's next, a trip to the art museum because she can't go an hour without a dose of culture? And no one should let herself go like that. Look, she can hardly . . . What?"

Iris turned, stomped up to her sister and growled at Mona through gritted teeth. "Are you kidding me? You're one to talk about silly and frivolous. You've never lifted a finger to do anything for yourself in your life, and you're breathing hard after walking a hundred yards." She realized she was waving her arms around and fearing she'd send her phone flying, she slipped it into the pocket of her slacks. "Maybe you should go back inside with all those other fashionistas before the breeze musses your gorgeous coiffure."

Mona put a hand to the side of her head and looked pained. Iris would have laughed if she weren't so mad. Was her vain sister really that worried about her hair? Unbelievable. She seized the moment of weakness to give her sister a piece of her mind.

"For your information, Emily is brilliant. She rose through the ranks at Boeing to become head of a technical division by the time she retired. Amanda taught art at the University of Washington. She still shows in galleries." Iris stopped for a moment to catch her breath and found she still had more to say. "But you . . . you who have never done anything in your life but tell other people that what they are doing is wrong, you showed up at my door this morning and tagged along with us. But you can't even just tag along like a decent human being, you have to spend the entire morning lecturing us on the right way to shop, the right way to drive, the decor of the restaurant, how to tell a story. I don't even know what the hell you're doing here. So just shut up and leave me alone."

Iris turned her back and put it into high gear, leaving her cursed sister in the dust. When she caught up with Emily and Amanda they were arguing over what variety the trees were that ringed the parking area. She smiled and joined them. Amanda looked at her and put an arm around her shoulder.

"Why are you shaking, Iris?"

"Oh, it's just Mona. She's had this effect on me all my life."

Emily and Amanda turned around to look back at Mona. Against her will, Iris turned too, and sighed at what she saw. Mona was standing at the edge of the sidewalk, hand still on her head and tilting slightly to one side. Then she took a breath, turned slowly around and started walking back the way they'd come.

"My asthma is acting up," Amanda said. "Listen to me wheezing. It must be the pollen. Mona," she called, "wait up. I'll walk back with you."

Emily fanned herself with her visor. "No, walking was a bad idea. I'm sorry I dragged you all out here. It's too hot. We'll all go back in with Mona."

Amanda was now at Mona's side, chatting away and threading the taller woman's hand through her arm with a pat. Iris was surprised to hear Mona ask Amanda if she was a fiber artist. "I just thought, because of your knitting."

Amanda laughed. "No, I work in oils. Knitting is just a hobby. I'm not very good at it. But I do buy hand spun yarns. I love the colors and textures."

Iris trailed along after them tamping down a nauseating mix of guilt and a sense of righteous accomplishment.

"Let's go grab lunch," said Emily as they reached the door.

Amanda laughed. "Emily, sometimes I think you only come to the casino for the food."

"And the drink," said Emily. "Don't forget the drink. We get free drinks starting at eight tonight." She did a little jig. "I plan to have at least two."

At the entry to the café, Mona begged off. "I'm just not hungry. I'll get a sandwich later. I'll be in the casino. It seems to be my lucky day."

Iris frowned at the depressed tone under the sarcastic comment. Mona looked pale and subdued. She hadn't eaten her breakfast and now she wasn't hungry? She'd never had that effect on her older sister before. Mona had always been the one who could devastate Iris with a sharp word, or a judgmental tilt of her head.

"Is she okay?" Amanda asked. "She looks paler than she did this morning. And she seemed to be quite wobbly when we were walking. I had to hold her arm."

"We had words," said Iris. "She's not used to me telling her off. I'm sure she'll be fine." Iris didn't feel as brave as she tried to sound. True, standing up to Mona for once had produced a surge of pride. But she also felt mean watching her sister slowly wander toward the sound of the bells, all alone and looking so old. Mona had been acting a little strangely at times. Perhaps she really did need to talk to Iris about something. Maybe Iris should have listened. She'd been quite unkind, launching into that diatribe.

No, she told herself, that is just your lifelong habit of trying to get along. She would not let Mona manipulate her into feeling guilty about saying what she felt for once. She shook off the worry and followed Amanda and Emily into the restaurant. She'd find

Mona after lunch and ask what she wanted. Most likely another small loan, which Iris would be happy to give her.

CHAPTER 5

"Emily, stop. Don't make me laugh," said Iris, covering her mouth to avoid spewing chocolate cake across the table.

"Oh, my, all this iced tea has gone right through me," She put down her napkin. "I need to use the girls' room. Be right back."

Amanda and Emily both nodded, their mouths full of food. As she walked away, Iris thought of Mona again. She'd have loved the stories Emily told about her insane birding buddies. If only she would listen without having to pick people apart. After she'd finished here she would go back and order Mona a sandwich and take it out to the casino as a peace offering.

A whooping and yelling distracted her from her thoughts. Some lucky duck must have won a jackpot.

As she was washing her hands, Iris noticed she needed a fresh coat of lipstick. She reached for the front pocket of her little cross body purse. The purse wasn't there. For a moment she stood looking at the confusion on her face in the mirror. She patted herself all over, but found no purse, only her cell phone in her pocket. What was it doing in her pocket? She always kept it in the front pocket of her purse. Then she remembered she'd bought that beautiful new shoulder bag. But that bag was not on her shoulder.

Sighing at her forgetfulness, she went back to the stall, thinking she must have hung it on the hook behind the door. But it wasn't there. Was this the right stall? She checked the others and didn't find it in those either. The last stall was in use. Standing in front of the closed door, she cleared her throat.

"Excuse me, dear." She cleared her throat again. "I'm sorry to bother you, but is there a bag hanging in there? Pale lavender leather? I've lost my bag."

"No, ma'am. The only bag in here is my Gloria swag bag."

"Oh? What is a Gloria swag bag?"

"The gift bag from Gloria Trammel. I got it at her Local Glory Brunch."

"I see," said Iris. Gloria. That was the name of the woman in pink. So she was giving out gifts. That would explain her popularity. "Well, thank you, dear. Now what the heck did I do with that thing?"

"Hope you find it."

Iris wandered toward the door and stood staring off into space, trying to remember. A whirring caught her attention and she looked around. Beside her a cascade of paper towels was pouring toward the floor. It looked like a paper waterfall. Oh, her shoulder was against the sensor. Embarrassed, she jumped away, but paper kept coming out. She tore the paper off, gathering it up in her arms before it could hit the dirty floor. Paper kept coming. She tore that off and added it to the wad in her arms then whacked at the machine trying to stop it. This only seemed to make it worse. Anxious to escape technology run amok, she gave up and ran to the door, using the loose end of the wad to grasp the germy door handle. If she hadn't lost her purse she could fold this paper up to save for later. It would come in quite handy, and she hated waste.

43

A burst of applause and laughter greeted her as she opened the door. There seemed to be a lot of people out there. Iris cringed. A casino was a bad place to lose a purse. So many people were out for the quick score and feeling lucky. Not that she'd ever had trouble in all the years she'd been coming here. But judging from the movies, not everyone in a casino could be trusted. She had a lot of cash in that bag today, all her play money. Tears welled in her eyes as she stood in the foyer looking around, the wad of paper towels clutched in her arms, wondering what she could have done with that bag and searching for a trash can.

The noisy knot of people clustered in front of the reception desk caught her attention. Mostly women, they were the source of the hilarity and cheers she'd heard earlier. They were all dressed to the nines, much like that Gloria what's-her-name.

She pulled her gaze from them and considered what to do next. The hotel must have a lost and found. She would report the loss to the front desk person, and also tell them about the faulty paper towel machine. But that was quite a line to have to stand in. Oh, well. If you can't keep track of your belongings there is always a price. She shrugged and headed toward the crowd to fight her way to the desk.

Oh, no. There was that awful blond woman again. She was posing for a photograph with her arm around a fawning younger woman. Gloria had a huge false smile pasted on her face. The photo done, she turned and whispered theatrically in the ear of a distinguished looking man. Iris wondered, idly, if he was the one she'd seen the woman kissing. Iris, having no desire to get anywhere near those two looked for a the best way to get past the swarm. But just then Gloria started herding all the women into a line right across Iris' path. She stopped to see what was happening.

"Time for the unbagging video, ladies," Gloria said, holding up her phone. All the women started chattering again. "Get ready."

The fans all smiled and raised glossy pink paper totes with the word Gloria! emblazoned on the side in flourishing gold script. "And now for our unbagging," Gloria said in a theatrical voice. "Look at all the Glorious gifts my attendees have received today." The women each reached in and pulled out an item. "Jasmine has a tube of Ogle's Insta Mascara. And look at that luscious Hashtag brand scarf Katie has draped around her neck. Silk, of course. What has Lorelei found? A gorgeous tube of Influencer Lipstick, in Plummet. And Yolanda has my favorite, the must-have sunglasses of the season from Wiley Posner." The litany went on and on, with woman after woman pulling another item from the bag and posing with it. But Iris had seen enough. That phrase "must-have" grated on her every time she heard it. The fashion industry was always harping on about women expressing their individuality with one breath, and with the next proclaiming that everyone must have the same of something else. Handbags were the biggest must-have, it seemed, and looking at these women it was clear they had all got the memo. They all had similar purses decked out with a lot of rings and hardware draped over their shoulders. And if that was the must-have style for this season, it could, by definition, not be the must-have style for next season. So would all these miles of leather and pounds of metal end up in the landfill next month to make way for the winter season must have. Really, what were people thinking following all these trends? The world was going to hell in a handbag.

Disgusted, Iris turned, aiming to make a wider arc around the obnoxious group, and stopped with a jolt. There was her bag. It was sitting right there on the end of that console table.

With a squeak of joy, she hurried over to retrieve it. What a ninny, why had she left it there? In this light she saw that Emily was right, it was less lavender than pink. Vowing never to let it out of her sight again, she clasped it to her bosom. Shoving the wad of paper towels under one arm, she slung the bag onto her shoulder, and almost weak with relief, headed back to the restaurant. It was awfully heavy. She'd have to clean it out later, but right now she just needed to get back to her friends.

There went that small man in the security uniform again. The one she'd seen fooling with the electric cables. There was a second one, almost identical, right behind him. He must be the one Amanda had seen. Iris smiled at them, and they nodded to her. What it was about them that seemed so odd?

She was jolted out of her reverie by someone yelling and whooping again. Another jackpot? Wow. This was a really lucky day. She felt a little thrill of anticipation, mixed with irritation that she wasn't out there playing. Drat! She wanted to win a jackpot, too. She had to get back out to the casino floor.

The yelling kept up, and now she noticed it was coming from behind her this time, from the gaggle in the foyer. Turning to see what they were up to now, Iris saw the fancy dressed blond woman looking over the heads of the women around her. The woman glared in her direction with a face that looked like murder. Then she looked down and gave another one of those terrible faux smiles as the group broke into more applause and held up their cell phones to take still more pictures The small men in uniform had stopped and were gazing toward the blond, who stretched up tall again as if on tiptoe and seemed to be having some kind of fit. Her head was jerking sideways. Iris stared at her. Then she saw one of the little men, and then the other, turn from the woman and look straight into Iris' eyes. She looked behind her. What were they looking at? There was no one

"Are they looking at me?" she said aloud as she took a step backward.

Iris' mind flew back to Amsterdam, the dark alleys, the hulking man who had followed her. She didn't wait around to see what these two wanted – she fled toward the casino. It was a total maze. If they chased her she could lose them in there.

46

She looked back and sure enough, they were right behind her, coming fast. The blond woman was once again smiling and gushing at her fans. Then she looked toward Iris again with a gaze that pierced her like a laser.

Iris ran faster around the bank of slot machines, tossing the wad of paper towels aside as she went. It was a waste of paper, but it was just slowing her down.

She ducked into an alcove between two banks of slot machines to catch her breath. There was one good thing about being short. They couldn't see her over the tops of the slots. The two men came around the corner after her, but one of them slipped on the wad of paper and went down hard. There were gasps and a wave of laughter. The poor guy – people were so mean. The other man kicked the paper to the side and helped his friend up, and they took off running again. Iris watched them go, sneaked out of her hiding place, doubled back the way she had come and out the nearest door to the parking lot. Dashing between cars, she got as far from the building as she could and then stopped beside a big SUV, bent over with her hands on her knees and breathed.

When she had her wind back she looked around. This was not where they had parked. The lot was vast and she groaned at the impossibility of finding her car. Then she saw a sign with an arrow pointing to valet parking. At least she knew which way to go.

***

"Where the heck is Iris?" Emily had been tapping her spoon against the plate under her empty banana split bowl for several minutes.

"You know," said Amanda, who was ready to knock the spoon out of her hand, "these things can take a while."

"Don't I know it. But she's been gone ten minutes. I wonder if she's okay."

"There were a lot of women in there earlier. Perhaps there's a line. Let's give her five more minutes. Besides, we have to wait for the sandwich I ordered for Mona." Amanda returned to enjoying the last bite of her apple pie. "Have another cup of tea."

"Not on your life. I'll be in the same state as Iris if I do." Emily resumed clinking her spoon until the sandwich arrived.

"Okay, this is beyond ridiculous. Let's go find her. I've got her bag here." Emily patted the lavender tote sitting beside her on the seat. "At least I think it's Iris'. Hers is the lavender one right?"

"Yes. Mine is yellow, Mona's is peach, Iris' is lavender. You really should have got one. That blue was lovely."

"And add to this lost bag muddle? I don't think so. You were crazy to get them all the same." Amanda and Emily paid the bill and were heading out the restaurant door, just as a blur shot past down the hall.

"Was that Iris?" asked Amanda, peering around a potted palm. "That was Iris." The two watched their friend's retreating back. "And now we know that isn't Iris' bag after all. See, she has hers on her shoulder. So this one must be Mona's." She opened her own bag and put the sandwich inside. "I wonder what she's doing with that wad of paper towels."

"Whoa, well excuse me," said Emily snarkily to the young man in uniform who nearly plowed her down.

"Sorry, ma'am," he called over his shoulder as he and his companion race walked away.

"Excuse me, sir," he said, sidestepping a man with a walker.

"Those two are going to hurt someone," said Emily.

"That was the fellow I saw in the ladies' room this morning," Amanda said, staring after the uniformed pair.

"Where is everyone going in such a hurry?" said Emily.

"I assume Iris must be going to find Mona. I knew she was anxious to get back to the casino, but I didn't know she was that anxious. Let's join them, I'm feeling much better and I'm ready to take another spin on a few of those machines. I'm with Mona, I think this is my lucky day."

Emily's eyes were wide as she turned to look at her friend. "Did you miss the fact that Mona was being facetious?"

"How could you tell that? You don't even know her."

"I thought artists noticed details."

"Oh, I do abstracts. I notice shapes, colors, plays of light."

"Okay," said Emily. "That explains a lot. Lucky you. No dealing with reality." She swept a hand toward the casino. "Lead the way toward your future riches."

CHAPTER 6

Mona didn't know what to do now. She'd put one dollar into a machine and won a jackpot just like that. It was impossible, but it had happened.

The elation and excitement and unreality of suddenly winning a pile of money had almost done her in. Unable to breathe, she had barely managed to sign her name on all those forms, she shook so badly. Now she was feeling lightheaded and tired and really needed to sit down again. Her empty stomach twisted painfully. Maybe she should try to get a little something down. The cafe might have a broth, or even juice. Tomato juice sounded really good.

The jangling mechanized music was getting to her, too. Hurting her head, and the nerves all over her body. She should have tried to eat something when the others went for lunch. If only she hadn't been so upset with Iris. That had made the stomachache worse. But on the other hand, if she'd gone with them she would have missed out on winning a quarter of a million dollars.

She grinned. What a thrill. She'd never felt anything like it. Not that she'd see that much. She'd taken the one-time, lump sum, cash option, as there was no point in choosing the gradual payout. Still, a lot of money. She was dumbfounded at her luck. Though it would have been nice if it had come a bit sooner.

Woozily, she started toward the nearest bank of slot machines. Those nice high stools were the closest place to rest and think about whom she should give the money to. Her daughter, of course. But Carrie hadn't spoken to her in ten years. Iris didn't really need the money. She'd been giving Mona loans for this and that ever since Mona's last divorce. She couldn't think of any charity that she really cared . . .

A cloud of fragrance wafted past in the wake of a dozen well-dressed women. There seemed to be an awful lot of fashionable young women here today. Something must be going on. She watched another trio clad in designer fashion drift by laughing and chatting. Oh, those were nice shoes. She pined for the day when she could still wear stilettos. But her poor old feet. She was paying for all those years of wearing pointed toes. These youngsters would pay someday too.

What were those men doing? They were staring at her, whispering. Were they trying to steal her money? Her hard-earned winnings? The first thing she'd ever won in her life? They'd better not if they knew what was good for them. Perhaps they were her security detail. If so, the people in the cashier's office should have notified her.

She clamped her arm down more securely on her purse. It was bulky and heavy, now that it was stuffed with cash. The faintness came over her again, her head spun and she nearly toppled off the stool. With an effort, she righted herself, smoothed her hair, and blamed the near faint on the rush of adrenaline that hit when she thought about how much money was in that bag.

After wandering all over the casino floor, peering between the clanging banks of machines, avoiding avid gamblers, cocktail waitresses, and flocks of supermodels, Emily and Amanda had still not found Mona or Iris. The casino was vast and Amanda could tell that Emily was getting peeved. This was going to take a while. And if their quarry were on the move, rather than sitting in one place staring at a monitor, it might take all afternoon to catch up with them.

"Maybe we should split up," said Amanda, stretching up on tiptoe to see across the tops of the glaring and blaring slot machines.

"And make it all worse? Over my dead body," Emily said. She pulled out her phone. "I'm going to call Iris. That's the only way we'll ever find them."

"You've got her purse."

"Oh, right." Emily ended the call. "Strange though. I didn't hear it ringing." She opened the bag and looked in all the pockets. "No phone in here."

"Oh look, there are those two little men again." Amanda pointed over top of the slot machines. "They're so cute." She giggled. "I still say it looks like they're plotting something."

The men were standing beside a row of slot machines and peering over them toward the cashier's window. They had their heads together and were whispering and watching something. Amanda beckoned to Emily and the two of them tiptoed up behind the pair so they could eavesdrop on what they were saying. Emily raised her phone and snapped their picture.

"I do, I think it's her."

"It does look like her. But . . ."

Amanda looked beyond the men to the woman they were talking about. It was Mona. Now that they mentioned it, Mona did look like Iris. Taller, better dressed, older, but other than that the sisters could almost be twins.

"I didn't think she was so tall. She seemed really short when I first saw her."

And wasn't she wearing pants?"

"I thought so. But old lady pants are sometimes so baggy they look like dresses. Though I could have sworn her pants were black. Not blue and orange striped."

"You're right. This can't be the same lady."

"But look at the bag, she's got the bag."

"Yes, I noticed the bag, though what color was Gloria's bag? I thought it was pinkish."

"You could call that pink. Well, maybe it was peach-ish."

"What are you two looking at?" said Mona to the men. Then she looked past them and saw Emily and Amanda. Her eyes narrowed.

"Emily, Amanda, why are you standing behind those men like . . ." Amanda turned around whistling tunelessly and looking at the ceiling. Emily motioned frantically for Mona to zip it and plopped into a chair in front of a slot machine.

"Hey now, what do you think you're doin'? You get out of here." The voice was harsh, raspy and very unfriendly. Amanda looked down and saw a wizened woman staring at Emily. Her eyes were bloodshot and she was holding a glass of beer. "That's my machine." The woman began coughing in Emily's face and waving her arms, sloshing beer over the rim of the glass. "Freeloaders are always trying to horn in. I been playing that machine all morning and I'm not gonna let you waltz in here and take winnings that are rightfully mine."

"Sorry, ma'am," said Emily, sliding off the seat and backing away.

Mona's voice trailed away, ". . .like you just lost all your money in that Lotus Blossom machine."

The men turned toward them and a little squeak escaped Amanda. She slapped her hand over her mouth. Emily ignored the men, smiled, grabbed Amanda by the shirtsleeve and pulled her around the men to stand beside the taller woman.

"Oh, hi Mona. I didn't see you there. How's tricks?" said Emily.

"Hi Mona," said Amanda, batting Emily's hand away. "What do you mean you didn't see her?"

"Shut up, Amanda," said Emily out of the corner of her mouth.

"Tricks? Um, tricks are good." Mona's eyes slid back and forth between Emily, Amanda and the two men. The men had backed off slightly, trying to get free of the old woman who had turned her wrath on them instead, and were scanning the rest of the casino. But they still had Mona in their sights.

"I . . . um . . . got you lunch," said Amanda, breaking into a too-big grin of her own.

"Are they gone yet?" said Emily between her teeth. Mona shook her head slightly, smiled wanly and put a hand to her head. "I'm ... I'm so glad to see you. It's been such a long time."

Mona seemed to be working to get control of herself and Amanda wondered if something had happened.

"I was just about to . . . uh . . . go outside and . . . I mean, for a smoke . . . want to come with me? We can catch up on what's been going on since last time we saw each other."

"Great, yes, you bet," said Emily. She grabbed Amanda by the sleeve again and started propelling her in the direction of the exit on the far side of the casino. Amanda tried to break away, but

Emily was strong. Maybe it was time to start going to water aerobics as Emily and Iris had been pestering her to do. Mona followed them. There were many banks of slots to wind past before they could get outside. They walked slowly at first, without speaking. Then Mona must have decided the silence was suspicious because she started to babble.

"I suppose I really should give up smoking. They say it's going to kill me someday. But I'm eighty years old. So I'm not too worried. Yet. Hah hah!"

Emily chuckled in a forced way.

"It's bad for my asthma," said Amanda with a little cough.

The men were still following them at a distance. Mona walked faster. Emily and Amanda hustled to catch up to her. The men kept following. Suddenly Mona jerked to her left, pulling Emily with her. Emily pulled Amanda, who yelped as she nearly tripped. At the end of the aisle, Mona went right, then left again, avoiding another cluster of beautiful women carrying shiny pink shopping bags emblazoned with the word Gloria! in gold script. Amanda looked back. The men were surrounded by a cloud of pink accessories, bouffant hair and shimmering lips, looking around them alarmed and saying, "Excuse me, excuse us ladies." Emily started to snicker and took out her phone again.

Mona rounded another bank of machines and made a beeline for the exit doors. Emily swung around after her, but Amanda, feeling like the last kid in a game of crack the whip, went wide and ended up lying across one of the stools. The wind went whooshing out of her in a wheezing rush. Her bag spilled open and a ball of red yarn skittered away down the aisle and between the feet of one of the men. He jumped, caught a toe, tangled in the yarn, and went sprawling. Emily helped Amanda up, grabbed her bag, and they set off after Mona again, Amanda still fighting to catch her breath.

The men were up, too, pulling the yarn away and chasing them in earnest this time. Emily jogged, dragging Amanda. The grip on the sleeve of her dress was either going to rip it or permanently wrinkle it. Amanda felt her chest tightening. She would have to stop soon. They were finally passing the last bank of machines before the door and freedom, when a cocktail waitress carrying a tray of drinks appeared. Emily zigged, let go of Amanda's arm and the waitress passed between them with a hip shimmy and a giggled, "Oh! Pardon me ladies."

"I'm sorry," said Amanda over her shoulder.

There was a tugging from her side and Amanda looked just in time to see a knitting needle fly out of her bag. Oh, her beautiful sweater! The stitches were unraveling.

Behind her she heard a scream and a crash. Chancing a glance over her shoulder she saw that the two men had collided with the young waitress. "Ow!" yelled someone. The waitress went sprawling backward and the two men toppled forward after her. All three ended up in a heap, while the drinks tray spun up in the air and came down in a cascade of coke and rum and beer all over them. Amanda gasped, then started to laugh, which made her cough. She and Emily must have blocked the men's view of the waitress as she came around the corner. While the waitress screeched at the men, Amanda and Emily summoned the last of their energy and scampered away.

Suddenly the Star Wars theme blared across the casino floor, clashing with the jangling bells and metallic hums of the slot machines. Emily jumped, grabbed Amanda again with one hand, shoved her phone into her pocket with the other and ran toward the door. Mona, leaning against the door, seemed to be helpless with laughter. Then, as Emily and Amanda arrived, she stood straighter, and with great effort, pushed the door open and the three friends escaped.

Outside, Emily pulled out her blaring phone. She looked at the screen, then motioning for the others to join her, hid in the bushes around the corner from the entry.

"Iris," she hissed, "where are you?"

"Iris is at the car. She sounds completely panicked," Emily said, then switched on speaker phone.

"This is ridiculous," said Mona, with effort . . .. "We're hiding in the bushes like children. I'm getting dirt on my shoes."

"If you were up to running across the parking lot we wouldn't have to hide from those guys. I guess this is what they mean by old age is not for sissies," said Emily.

"What are you talking about?" said her phone. "A page of pixies?"

Amanda eyed the taller woman. Her face looked very thin. Her eyes were closed again as if the activity had entirely worn her out. "Are you okay, Mona?"

"I need you all to come here. Quick," said Iris's voice from the phone. "We have to leave. Some men are after me. I need to call Amy. I need my daughter."

"Calm down, Iris. Everything will be okay." Emily gestured to Mona and Amanda, pointing in the direction of valet parking. "Give us directions to where you are. We're on our way."

"Telling the queen of anxiety to calm down, that's rich." Mona chuckled meanly, but she stood up straight, gripped her bag tighter and tottered along across the parking lot beside Emily.

Amanda, wheezing and shaking her inhaler, lagged slightly behind. She needed to get a good puff, but it was hard while jogging. They reached the car just as Iris started to back out. Heaving themselves inside, they struggled to close their doors before Iris peeled them off on an upcoming lamppost.

They'd almost reached the road out of the lot when one of the small, mustachioed men came running up beside the car and grabbed the passenger side mirror. All four of them screamed at once and Iris swerved back and forth. Emily started growling.

"Are you simply trying to dislodge him, Iris, or do I need to wrest the wheel from your hands before you crash and send us all to our deaths?"

Mona burst out laughing, then subsided back against her seat. "Don't make me laugh, Emily, I've got a headache."

"I'm fine, Emily," Iris said, "though if you two don't pipe down I'm going to throw you out the windows right after I lose this guy."

She gave the wheel a mighty jerk. Amanda heard the little man let out a yip as he lost his grip and toppled over.

"Wow. Nice job, Iris," said Mona. "I didn't know you had it in you."

"There's a lot you don't know about me, Mona," Iris said through gritted teeth. Clearly the earlier tension between the sisters had not abated.

"That was well executed," said Emily. She was looking out the back window. "He took quite a tumble. Looks like he got good and scraped up. I'm impressed."

"I heard a scream. Is he okay?" said Amanda, struggling to get up off the floor.

"Who cares how he is. I'm just trying to make sure we survive."

"Look out for that van!" yelled Mona, and Iris swerved into a secondary parking lane to avoid a collision. Clear of the van, Iris sped out onto the access road.

Amanda, who'd fallen sideways across the back seat again as Iris took the last turn, righted herself. "Wow Iris, you can really drive well when you try. But aren't you going awfully fast?"

"I have to jet. That black van is on my tail and that guy I threw off just got into it."

Amanda and the others all looked behind them.

"Who are those guys?" said Amanda.

"Why are they after you, Iris?" said Emily.

"I thought they were after me," said Mona.

Iris frowned across at her sister. "After you? They are after me. That awful woman who accosted the valet this morning sent them to chase me. She looked at me like she wanted me dead. I don't like her. I don't trust her. And I'm hoping those two she sent after me aren't professional killers."

Amanda gasped. "Killers? Oh my god. They've been chasing us all over the casino."

"Cripes," said Emily. "No way are those guys killers. Three old women just got away from them."

Mona burst out in a honk of a laugh, then groaned and subsided. Amanda looked her over. Something was wrong with Mona.

Emily was looking forward again and shouted in dismay. "No. No, Iris, don't get on the freeway."

"Too late," said Mona.

"What's wrong with the freeway?" said Iris, glancing in her rearview mirror. "Oh, no." She slammed on the brakes.

"Boeing first shift just ended," said Emily. "We could be stuck in this for hours."

"At least those guys can't catch up to us," said Mona, eyes riveted on the side mirror. "They're about eight cars behind. Oh there, a semi just cut them off. Perfect."

Amanda rummaged through the heap of stuff on the seat between her and Emily.

"Ow! Amanda, take it easy with those knitting needles, that's the second time you've impaled me today."

"Sorry Emily. I just wanted to get this."

She held a wrapped sandwich between the seats. "Here's that lunch I got for you, Mona. Now seems like a good time to eat it, since we're just creeping along slow and Iris doesn't have to play race car driver for a while."

"Thanks, Amanda." Mona looked like she was going to cry, as she took the plastic wrapped sandwich. "Some people are so thoughtful."

Amanda saw Iris grind her teeth. That was kind of a snide dig on Mona's part. But Iris kept her temper in check.

"Oh, look," she pointed ahead. "There's a police car. You could pull over, Iris, and tell the cop to arrest these guys who are following us."

"Arrest them? Why?" asked Emily, gazing at Amanda.

"For harassment . . . or reckless endangerment . . . or something. That hanging off the side mirror stunt must have been illegal, don't you think?"

"I swear, Amanda," said Emily. "Sometimes you make no sense at all. Imagine Iris pulling over and telling that cop to stop trying to sort out who's at fault for that accident and instead dust her side mirror for fingerprints."

"I'm just going to take this next exit and head for home another way," said Iris, pulling into the exit lane.

"No!" said Amanda, surprised to hear the same word shouted by the other two passengers at the same time. "We were safe in traffic where they couldn't get near us."

"You can't lead them to your house, Iris," said Emily. She seemed remarkably calm about it, in Amanda's opinion.

"We don't want those guys to know where we live," she wailed, gasping and unable to contain her fright.

"Amanda, calm down," said Mona. "Or is it your intent to get our excitable driver all stirred up again? For the love of . . ."

"Well then, what are we going to do?" Iris said, as she sped down the exit ramp and through an intersection. "We can't just drive around all day."

"You have to lose them, Iris," said Mona.

"Lose them?" Iris snorted, sounding slightly hysterical. "I'm lost myself. Does anyone even know where this road goes?"

CHAPTER 7

They were speeding down a long straight road that headed off into a forest. A few moments later she saw the van far behind in the rearview mirror. "There don't seem to be any side roads to lose them on. And no place to turn around."

"There's not even a shoulder on this road," said Amanda.

"Based on your maneuvers back there in the parking lot, I'd think you could execute an e-brake slide," said Emily. The others fell silent and looked at her.

"What's a bakeslight?" said Iris.

"Never heard of it," said Mona. Amanda took a hit off her inhaler.

"E – brake – slide. It's when you pull up on the emergency brake and whip the wheel around."

"You mean the parking brake? That's insane," said Iris. "It's down by my left foot. I can't even reach it with my hand."

"They're gaining on us," said Amanda. "You'll have to go faster Iris."

"I wish we had a gun," said Mona. "We could send a couple of warning shots across their bow."

"I've noticed you use a lot of marine metaphors," said Amanda, "but we don't have a gun."

"Ow!"Emily rubbed her thigh. "How about we throw your knitting needles at them. Maybe we can puncture a tire."

Amanda grabbed her bag. "No, you don't. I already lost one, and a ball of yarn. I need my needles. Throw something of your own. Your birding binoculars maybe."

"as if, said Emily. She took out her phone and opened the window. "I'm going to at least get their picture. By the way, Iris, I have your bag here. You don't happen to have a gun in here do you?"

"Nope, just her plastic bags," said Mona.

"Will you let up about the plastic . . . wait, I've got my bag here." She patted the bag that sat on the console between her and Mona. The bag slid forward and tipped over, sending bundles of money into Mona's lap.

"What the . . .?" Iris slammed on the brakes, and goggling at the money, let go of the wheel for a second.

"Iris!?"

Iris grabbed the wheel again and stomped on the brake as the car tipped and her head smacked against the window.

A long wail came from her side of the car. Heart hammering, she looked up to see the van flash by going the wrong way.

"Oh, my neck," said Mona.

"That wasn't an e-brake slide," said Emily, "but close enough. You turned us around. Go, go!"

Iris settled her spinning eyeballs and floored it, speeding back the way they'd come. In the rearview mirror she saw the larger vehicle come to a stop and slowly execute a many-point turn on the narrow road. Mona said nothing, simply sat staring at the money in her lap and holding her head.

"Are you okay, Sis? Did you hit your head?"

"No. Iris, where did you get this money? Did you steal it from me?"

"What? No. You don't have any money."

"This bag is pink. Wasn't yours . . ."

"Lavender," said Amanda. "Iris' bag is lavender."

Emily held up the bag she'd brought from the restaurant. Iris, looking at it in the rearview, then down at the one beside her, was entirely befuddled. But she didn't have time to look at bags and discuss color perception, because the van was coming after them again and in front of her lay another decision.

"Quick. Should I get back on the freeway?"

"No!" said all three passengers at once. She went straight, under the freeway and into yet another forest on the other side.

"This road is even narrower. Does anyone know where it goes?"

"Nope," said Emily, "but it turns up there a quarter mile or so. Maybe we can lose them if we can round the bend far enough ahead of them. Step on it."

"I am stepping on it. The car doesn't go any faster."

"That's what you get for buying a Honda," said Mona.

"When I bought it I wasn't planning to spend much time outrunning killers, Mona, so you can just shut it."

"Amanda, what are you doing?" said Mona.

"I didn't eat my yogurt at lunch."

"And you thought you'd eat it now?"

"Go faster, Iris," said Emily. "Downshift or something, they're gaining."

"Or you could just stop and give them the bag," Amanda said.

Iris choked. "Amanda, are you crazy? I've just discovered that the bag I thought was mine is full of money. And since I don't have mine, which means I'm guilty of theft. And I'm driving without my license. I don't want to get a ticket."

"That's what you're worried about? A ticket?" Mona turned a blank face to her sister.

"But they aren't police, are they?" asked Amanda, turning to look back again. "I thought they were armored truck guys. Why are armored truck guys after you?"

Iris frowned. "I guess because I stole someone's money."

"Armored truck guys don't care about that unless it's from their truck. This doesn't make any sense."

"Amanda, keep up, they aren't armored truck guards, they are casino security guards," said Emily.

"Casino security?" asked Iris, heart racing. "Emily, do you think it's because they think I stole someone's bag? Why would they send security guards after me unless they think I'm a thief?"

"But you didn't know, and so if you now know that you stole someone's bag by accident, why don't you pull over and give it to them?"

"You've all got it wrong. Those are not armored car guards, or security guards. They aren't anything official," said Emily. "Look at that beat up, windowless black van they're driving. They look more like serial killers."

Amanda gasped again. "Now that you mention it, I remember they are also too small to be guards. And remember, the one I saw in the restroom? He was wearing a fake mustache." She turned and looked back. "Who are those guys?"

Iris giggled. "Loan her your binoculars, Emily."

"You know, she's right in a way," said Mona. "We could just call the police. If they aren't police that would get them off our tail."

"Once again, I'd get arrested for the theft. And that guy might press charges for me nearly running him over, and this whole merry chase. I'm speeding and being reckless, and evading capture and . . ." her voice trailed away. Her thoughts had circled back to the scene in the foyer before she picked up her lost purse.

"You'll never believe this, girls, but I think this bag belongs to that terrible woman we saw this morning. I think this is her money. And I don't think she got it legally."

"Why would you say that? Where would she have got a bunch of illegal money?" asked Emily.

"No. She must have won a jackpot," said Mona.

"They had this big event going on," said Iris. "Did you see all those dressed-up women? They were fans of the blond woman from this morning. They were all there to get their picture taken with. Maybe the casino paid her for that."

"You've got tit backwards. The casino would charge her for having her event there, not pay her," said Emily.

"Well, then, she was giving out gift bags full of expensive stuff," said Iris. "Maybe this is the grand prize."

"But wasn't she the gambling commissioner's wife?" said Amanda. "I don't think she should do that in a casino he oversees. That sounds wrong."

They fell silent for a moment. Iris studied the van in the rearview mirror. It was slowly creeping up on her. There were still no side roads in sight. What could she do to get away from those guys?

"Hey!" she yelled as a crazy idea came to her.

"What?" Amanda squeaked, pressing a hand to her ample bosom. "Oh my god, you scared me shouting like that."

"I've got an idea. Emily, get one of my plastic bags. Fill it with Amanda's yogurt. I'll slow a bit so they get close . . ."

"You want me to fling a bag of yogurt at them?"

"What the hell, Iris?" Mona was looking at her with disbelief.

"If we're lucky it will splat all over their windshield and give us time to get away while they can't see."

"Never hurt to try, I guess." Emily grabbed the container out of Amanda's hand, popped it open and dumped the yogurt into the bag. She started to giggle. "Okay, Iris, put me in range." As she rolled down the window she began to laugh uncontrollably. Iris slowed slightly, letting the van get a little closer.

"I think you're going to have to get control of yourself or you'll have trouble aiming that thing," said Amanda.

Emily only laughed harder. "Aim? Who said anything about aim?" She leaned out the window, gave the bag a twirl and let if fly up in the air.

"Oh my god!" yelled Iris a second later. "It worked!"

"I got a picture," said Emily. "No one will believe it otherwise."

Iris pressed the gas pedal as hard as she could as she watched the van behind her lurch side to side. "Would you look at that. They're slowing down."

"The bag is plastered right over the driver's windshield." Amanda was laughing now, too. "The wipers are just smearing the yogurt back and forth."

"I'm dumbfounded." Mona was gazing at Iris with new respect. She held up her palm. "High five, Iris." Iris smacked her hand, laughing.

"Nice shot, Emily," said Iris.

"Thank you. Keep your eye's on the road. You've just about got it," said Emily. "There, you're around the bend and they can't see you. Find a side road and pull off."

"There are no side roads," said Amanda, "but there's another bend coming up. Keep going, Iris."

Iris kept going around bend after bend. The trees thinned out. Sometimes there were patches of clear-cut.

"You'd think there would be at least one logging road to pull off onto," said Mona.

"I don't know what good that would do, logging roads tend to be dead ends. I don't want to do the killer's dirty work for them."

"Look, I can see the water," said Amanda.

"Oh crap, there's a Y ahead. What do I do now? Which way?"

They'd come up over a hill and, sure enough, the trees opened up and ahead the road split. One branch led out onto a low bluff, overlooking Puget Sound. The other road continued on through more trees.

"I remember now. That's the end of the road," said Emily. "I've been to this beach. That leads to the parking lot. I'd love to go to the beach right now. I could check for dead birds."

Mona groaned.

"Oh, no, no, no," Amanda was shaking her head . . . "We do not want to get stuck in there. Turn around quick, Iris, before they get here."

"Choose one, Iris," Mona said weakly.

"Hurry up, Iris, before they catch up again!" Amanda was wheezing.

"To the beach," said Emily.

"To the forest," said Amanda.

Iris floored it again, trying to follow directions, but in such a panic that she couldn't decide. The car jerked from side to side with her indecision. Everyone started yelling. Then the car jerked up and down and, amid much screaming, came to a rocking, bumping stop. The engine ground on something, knocked for a moment and quit. They were surrounded by silence and the soft green light of sun filtered through leaves .

"What the fuck?" said Amanda. Six shocked eyes turned her way and she flushed scarlet.

"I'm sorry," said Iris, panting. "I . . . I . . . I . . . is everyone okay?"

"Quiet." The hubbub died at Emily's command.

"What's that?" whispered Iris. Blood was pounding in her ears, but there was another sound, too.

"That's the van going by," said Emily. "We must be hidden by all this shrubbery. By god, Iris. You probably killed your car driving off the road like that, but I think you lost them."

"Well, how about that."

"Genius move, Sis. Congrats on losing the bad guys. What now?" asked Mona, wiping her mouth with the back of her hand.

"Um, we're going to need a tow truck," said Amanda.

"I've got triple A," said Iris. "Give me a moment to collect myself and I'll call them."

"Anyone know where we are?" said Mona. "I'm not from around here. So, not my circus."

"Surely they can track the car, or our cell phones, or something," said Amanda.

Emily sighed and put a hand over her face. "All our phones have mapping apps. We'll figure it out." She opened her door, batted away torn leaves and struggled through the branches. "Oh, listen, that's a pileated woodpecker. I need my binocs."

Mona burst out laughing, then stopped and put a hand to her head again.

Iris scanned her sister's face. "Why do you keep doing that, Mona? Did you hit your head this time?"

"For the last time, no. I didn't hit my head. Iris, it's time you told us where all this money came from."

"It was just in my purse. I have no idea who could have put it there. I have to use the restroom."

"Be my guest," said Mona, sweeping a hand toward the vegetation. "At least you have something besides hundred dollar bills to wipe with."

Emily and Amanda laughed.

Iris grabbed for her purse. "Don't be silly. I have tissues and all sorts of things in here," but the bag came up empty.

"Nope," said Mona, "only money."

"How many times do I have to tell you, your purse is back here?" Emily thrust the lavender bag toward Iris. "You left it in the restaurant and I brought it for you. If you hadn't been so hell bent on stealing somebody else's bag we wouldn't be in this mess."

Iris was dumbfounded. She stared at the two bags. "How . . . why . . . whose . . ."

"Exactly what we all want to know, Iris," said Mona.

Iris recovered and pulled the tissue packet out of her lavender purse. "I really have to pee." She opened the door, shoved the tissues into her jacket pocket and started clearing a path through the branches.

"I'll be right here," said Mona, leaning back and closing her eyes. "You all do whatever you want."

"Can I have a couple of tissues, Iris?" said Amanda climbing out behind her. "I feel the call of nature, too."

"This is going to take a while, isn't it," said Mona. "Wake me up when you get it sorted out."

Iris pulled out some tissues, handed them to Amanda, put her bag on the seat, and headed off into the bush. "We can figure this out when I get back."

It had taken Iris a long time to find a suitable place. By the time she got clear of the car and bushwhacked into a space open enough to turn around, she was drenched in sweat and doing a jig to keep from wetting her pants. Once upon a time she'd thought nothing of having to tinkle in the woods. But that was a hundred years ago, when Amy was a baby. Her almost-eighty-year-old thighs were just not up to squatting any more. She found a downed branch big enough to support her weight. Then she struggled back toward the car.

When she heard Emily yelling from a different direction, she realized she'd gone the wrong way and adjusted course. It seemed further on the way back, but finally she glimpsed a glint of sunlight off metal through the trees. She staggered toward it, bursting out of the brush to find herself on the side of the road looking up at the van that had been following them.

The two men were wrestling Amanda into the back. Her hands were tied and her face was ashen. She appeared to have fainted and her breath came in rasps. Iris quickly recovered from her shock, but was torn – save her friend or save herself? She looked back at the woods, then returned her gaze to the struggling men. Her eyes locked with the one inside the van. Oh, shit.

"Emily, Mona, help! They've got Amanda! Grab the tire iron, knitting needles . . . bring the gun!" And then the man got out of the vehicle and started toward her and she could see inside. Too late, all three of the women were trussed up in there like cord wood.

Heart hammering, she turned and struggled back into the bushes, hoping to get lost in the foliage. Staying free was her only hope to save her friends. But the men were on her in a flash. One held her arms, while the other tried to bind her feet. She danced around from foot to foot trying to make it hard for him and screaming, "No! No!"

This was just like Amsterdam again, when the thugs captured that old man on the street. And like at the Giant's Causeway when two other thugs had hijacked the shuttle at gunpoint. Why did everyone always go along quietly? That was not gonna happen this time. Iris' blood boiled. She was so done with thugs.

"No!" She screamed. "Noo. No, you don't!" What was it with men wanting to kidnap people all the time? "No!" She kicked and got one in the stomach. He went, "Oof," and toppled over backward, but the other one held on and, in another instant, her ankles were bound and they were lifting her into the van despite her thrashing and shouting "No!" at them again and again. "For god's sake, take it easy. I'm almost eighty years old, you beasts." Then they tied her wrists so tight that she couldn't struggle any more without injuring her sore shoulder.

She kept yelling, though, until Emily said from below her, "I don't think there's anyone out here to hear you, Iris."

The door slammed and the engine started. From the other side of the van Mona chuckled, then said weakly, "If an old lady screams the same thing over and over again in the woods where no one can hear her, is she still senile?"

CHAPTER 8

They all lay quiet, thinking their own private thoughts as the van rumbled along. Finally Emily broke the silence.

"I'm sure glad you two used the forest facilities back there. I don't have to worry about anything trickling down onto me. But you're deuced heavy."

"I can try to roll off," said Iris.

"Aahhrr, stop, that's worse."

Amanda and Mona said nothing.

"Where do you suppose they're taking us?" Iris whispered.

"Their lair, no doubt," said Emily. "To have their way with us. Amanda, you sound awful. Where's your inhaler?" There was no response. "Amanda?"

"I think she's out cold," said Iris. "They must have hit her on the head. How are you doing, Mona?"

"In the refrigerator, Grandpa," said Mona in a slow, slurred voice.

"What? Is that some kind of in-joke? I don't get it." There was no response.

"What's she talking about, Iris?"

"No idea."

Iris was very concerned about Mona. But for the moment, other things were more pressing. Even where the men were taking them paled in importance when she asked herself why. Why had the men chased them? Because she'd grabbed a purse full of money. But why was there so much money in that purse? Why hadn't the men just taken the bag from her? Why had they taken four old women captive? The whole thing was quite chilling. She shivered.

"Aaaahhh." The sound came from Amanda. "My . . . chest . . . hurts."

"Oh, Lord." Iris' face went cold with fear. "No heart attacks now, Amanda."

"Is . . . just . . . asthma . . . inhal . . . er."

"Where do you keep it? I can try to roll over and reach it."

"Jacket . . . pock . . . et."

"I think I feel it," said Emily. "It's the hard thing that's been digging into the side of my neck."

"You've taken a lot of doses today, it seems to me," said Iris. "How many are safe?"

There was no answer.

"Hey," shouted Iris, scrabbling around behind her, trying to locate the inhaler. "You've got a sick woman back here."

"Stop. That tickles," said Emily.

"She needs her asthma medication or she's going to asphyxiate." Iris' fingers bumped against something lying on the floor. It moved slightly. Slowly, painfully, she worked at that tube

74

and finally managed to hook a finger around it and gather it into her palm.

There was no response from the front seat. Surely they could hear her just fine. She was only three feet away. Iris was getting pissed. She shouted louder.

"How can you just keep on driving when a woman is dying in the back of your van?"

There was whispering from the front of the vehicle, but no change in the motion.

"At least one of us is going to asphyxiate," said Emily, sounding worse than Amanda ever had.

Then the van slowed and Iris felt a surge of relief. They were going to help Amanda.

But instead, the driver made a series of turns, left, right, right, right, left and came to a stop. There was a squeal and a grind and the van moved slowly forward again. She recognized that sound. A garage door opening. Oh, shit.

A few minutes later Iris, sweaty and breathing heavily, was standing, very much against her will, in a small bedroom and blinking in the light of a high window. Her ankles were still bound with some kind of tape, and she was hopping mad at the indignity of being dragged down the hall.

She'd stood there looking around and noticed she still had the thing she'd picked up clutched in her hand. It felt like a small bottle. She pulled her hands around as far as she could to her side and looked down. Emily's bottle of hand sanitizer. Great. That was a huge help in their present predicament. At least they could die germ-free. She managed to drop it into her jacket pocket just as the door opened and Emily was dragged in and dumped.

Pushing her shoulder against the wall, Emily struggled to her feet, still shouting that they were in violation of the Constitution, her civil rights and the Americans with Disabilities Act.

"What are they doing with the others?" Emily asked, hopping a few feet and putting her ear to the door. Iris was worried. By the time the van had stopped, Amanda was hardly breathing and Mona hadn't said another incoherent word. When the van door opened, she'd been hauled out of the vehicle and stood up on her bound feet in a garage full of boxes. The men had dragged her down a hall and into this room and shut the door. A moment later they'd brought Emily. Then, nothing more.

"Do you hear anything?"

"No. Wait. Yes. Scraping. Some grunting." Emily jumped back from the door just as it flew open and a chair burst through. The door slammed again.

Mona was tied to the chair, her head lolling. She moaned. "Mama. My head."

Iris hopped over to her. Turning her back, she clawed at the strand of packing tape that the men had loosely wrapped to hold her sister to the back of the chair and finally managed to break it.

"Mona honey, wake up now."

"It's all in your head. They . . ." something garbled, " . . . say that."

"Emily, help me get my hands undone." Iris hopped over to Emily and turned her back. "They must have run out of rope after they did our wrists."

"They're coming again." They both turned to the door. It opened again and Amanda stumbled in. Her legs weren't taped. The door slammed once more. Iris heard a lock and then the sound of voices, but she couldn't hear words.

"Your hearing is better than mine, Emily, can you tell what they're saying?" She eyed Amanda, who swayed slightly, but seemed to be breathing better.

"No. But it sounds like there are women here."

"Maybe their wives or girlfriends. That's good, women will be nicer to us," said Iris.

Emily shrugged and turned to Amanda. "Amanda, are you okay, dear? Let's find that inhaler."

"One of the men took it. But one of them also helped me take a dose. I'm okay now." She rolled her head, then her shoulders. "That was a brutal ride. I hurt everywhere."

"Hah, you should try being the one on the bottom," said Emily. "I've got permanent bruising from you two pressing me into the floor."

"Let's get out of these bonds," said Iris, backing up toward her two friends. "Can someone reach the knots on my wrists? My shoulder is about to pop out of the socket."

For a few minutes they worked on the cords. Though she couldn't see what she was doing, Iris finally managed to get Emily's wrists free. A second later Emily had freed the rest of them. Amanda stroked Mona's cheek while Emily and Iris untaped their ankles.

"What happened? How did they capture you and Mona?"

"I'm not sure. We were just sitting there waiting for you and Amanda to come back. I was looking for a tow truck company to come get us out. Next thing I knew I was on the ground with the wind knocked out of me, a wad of leaves in my mouth, and my hands tied. They must have realized we'd gone off the road and doubled back. Maybe they heard Mona and me arguing about whether or not to go back to the casino and return the money. Your sister is a piece of work, Iris."

"I know. I take it she wanted to keep the money."

"Yep. Have you two always been criminals?"

"I'm not a criminal, I just thought the bag was mine. It was an honest mistake. I don't know about Mona's relationship to the law. We haven't spent much time together since we were kids. Just the obligatory holiday get-togethers."

They helped Mona out of the chair and laid her on the bed. Emily checked vital signs while Iris spoke softly into her ear. "You're going to be fine, Sis. You probably just need some food. Did you eat that sandwich?" Mona didn't respond.

"She opened it. I saw her. But, now that you mention it, I didn't see her take a bite. It looked really good. I got the meatloaf one because that's what I was going to get if I didn't have the fish and chips. Which were excellent by the way. If we go back there you should . . ."

"Amanda, will you quit babbling, please?" Mona rolled on her side and sat up. "I'm fine."

"You're not fine," barked Emily. "Your heart rate is elevated and you're very pale."

Iris motioned to Emily to back off. "Let me talk to Mona alone for a minute."

"Fine, I'll go hammer on the door and holler that I need the bathroom." Emily went off and did that.

Iris struggled down to kneel on the floor beside the bed. "Honey, I think you need to lie down a while longer. Besides what Emily said about your heartbeat, you were incoherent in the van, and then went nearly catatonic. Is there something you're not telling me?"

Mona sighed and lay back down. Her hand went to her head again. "I've been trying to talk to you, but every time I do something goes wrong or you get mad at me. I'm not very good at family stuff."

That was an understatement. Mona had been divorced three times and alienated her only daughter so badly the two hadn't spoken since Carrie graduated high school. "Well things have gone about as wrong as they can, so go ahead and tell me now."

Mona chuckled, then choked on her laughter and started coughing. "No, Iris, things are going to get worse very soon. I'm sorry. I should have stayed home."

Iris sat back, frowning down at Mona's pale face. "What do you mean things are going to get worse?"

"I'm dying, Sis. I mean, I already was, but I think our adventure this afternoon has hastened things along. I can feel it. I'm nauseous and dizzy and very, very tired." Mona lay her hand over her right eye. "I can't see properly. It's a tumor. Inoperable."

Iris paused. Health scares were one of the ways Mona had got attention over the years. But at eighty it very well could be real this time. "Oh, Mona, I'm so sorry. How long have you known about this? Why didn't you tell me?"

"It was pretty sudden. I started having bad headaches about a month ago. I went to the doctor two weeks ago and they found the tumor right away. It's big and it's moving fast. I had to quit doing a lot of things. When it started to affect my speech and balance last week, I knew I had to come see you one last time."

"To ask me to forgive you for all your bullying and bad behavior?"

"No, to get in a few last licks," said Mona, with a grunting laugh. "Of course to apologize and ask forgiveness, you idiot."

It was Iris' turn to laugh. She shook her head ruefully. "Your technique is impeccable. Who wouldn't want to forgive you?"

"Well, Carrie for one. She hasn't returned my calls."

Iris dropped her head and closed her eyes. "You were pretty rough on her."

"I know. But look how tough she turned out. Have you Googled her lately? She's done very well for herself, so I try not to regret the way I raised her."

"I don't know that I'd go that far. She may be doing fine with her security business and her life, but your own daughter absolutely hates you. That's not a good thing, Mona."

"I know, I know." Mona closed her eyes and swallowed with some effort. "My mouth is really dry. It's too late to do anything about Carrie. She learned the lessons I wanted to teach her. Kids have to know that they cannot rely on anyone else. They have only themselves. They can't rely on friends, family, even their own mothers. Everyone looks out for themselves, always. And anyone who doesn't learn that turns out like you, Iris, so trusting you get taken at every turn."

"Mona, that is an awful thing to say. I do not get taken."

"You do. You got taken by Glen, that shit of a husband of yours."

"His name was Ken," Iris hissed between her teeth. "And he was a good man."

"Right. Look at that shithole little house and the bills he left you with. In that shithole neighborhood. And what are you doing for fun today? Going to a shithole casino to get taken. With friends who don't really like you and whom you don't really like. It's just convenient for you to use each other."

Iris silently glared at her sister. "Are you trying to get me to strangle you so you don't have to go through the long process of dying from a brain tumor? I'm not going to sit here and listen to this abuse, even if you are dying." Iris started to get up, but Mona grabbed her wrist.

"This is just my kind of love, Iris. I'm trying to help you. You have to see things clearly. Everyone is out for themselves. Until you understand that, you will continue to be a victim. The only thing you can trust other people to do is hurt you."

"Mona, I don't understand how we grew up in the same house. Mom and Dad were kind to . . ."

Mona interrupted. "To you, Iris. They were not kind to me. Whether it was because I was the oldest and you were the baby, I don't know. But they treated us very differently."

"Because you were trouble and I was compliant."

"You think compliance is an inborn trait or something? They gave you things to make you compliant."

"They gave you things, too. Why didn't you comply?"

"I always saw what they were doing. I took the things they gave, but didn't let those things trap me into doing what they wanted. That's called coercion, or more bluntly, slavery."

"And that attitude is what's called being a selfish, ungrateful bitch!"

"Iris!" Amanda looked shocked.

"Shhhh," said Emily. "I'm trying to hear what the men are saying and you two bickering is making that very hard."

"You must be feeling better, Mona," said Amanda.

"Yes, Amanda, absolutely. I'm fit as a fiddle." Mona sat up again and this time managed to put her legs over the side of the bed and her feet on the floor. Using the chair for support, she got to her feet. "I'm all ready to help you plan our escape."

CHAPTER 9

"Right," said Emily. "We have to come up with a plan to get out of here."

"If there were sheets on the bed, we could rip them up and make a rope to climb out the window," said Amanda. "Darn, they took my bag with the scissors."

"The romantic words of a true fiber artist," said Mona. "It would be funny to watch you rip up sheets though. Especially since it would be entirely in vain. We're on the first floor."

"How do you know that?" asked Iris.

"Did you go up any stairs to get here from the garage?"

"I didn't notice . . . Oh. Of course, they dragged you here in the chair." Mona had been more with it than she let on. She always was good at subterfuge.

"That doesn't prove anything," said Emily. "The backyard might be a slope."

"I saw out the windows, I assure you. The house is a rambler. All one story."

"Who are these guys?" said Iris.

"I got pictures this time. Let's see if we recognize them." Emily pulled out her phone and they all gathered around. "Oh, that one's too blurry."

"What is that?" asked Amanda, turning her head this way and that. "Is that a picture of your fingers?"

"Turn it this way," said Mona, and then broke into cackling, uncontrolled laughter. "Beautiful shot Emily. That's the cocktail waitress' cleavage."

Emily turned bright red, pocketed her phone and changed the subject.

"The chair. We could ambush them when they come through the door. Hit them over the head with it."

"They're small men," said Amanda. "And it's four to two. We might be able to overpower them."

"So many grand ideas," said Mona, still laughing. "You could sit on them, Amanda. They'd never get up again."

"Mona!" said Iris. "That was completely uncalled for. Saying such a thing is awful, even for you."

"Whatever," said Amanda, waving a hand. "I'll do anything that's needed to get us out of here. Even admit I'm a little overweight."

"Oh, for god's sake," said Mona. "You're all missing the point. They may be small, but whoever these guys are, they're fifty years younger than any of us." She leaned forward and put her head in her hands. "We aren't strong or agile enough to take them on in hand-to-hand combat. We need a better plan than that. Maybe we could send Emily out to talk them to death."

"Mona!" Iris was aghast at her sister's remark.

"Stop it, the lot of you," Emily barked, glaring at Mona. "We're going to play the old lady card." A sly grin spread over her face. The others grumbled. "Complain all you want. You know it works every time."

"She's right," said Iris.

"Well, I'm not going to be the old one," said Mona.

"Not only are you old, you're the oldest one of the group," said Iris. "And you're sick to boot."

"Sick?" Amanda recoiled slightly.

"Shut up!" This time Emily succeeded in quieting everyone. Even the voices outside the door fell silent. She lowered her voice to a whisper, but still sounded dangerous. "I've had it with your bickering, you two. We'll all be old, okay?" She pointed at the center of the room and dropped her voice to a whisper. "Amanda, you fall down on the floor."

"What?" Amanda's eyes went wide and she whispered back. "I'll never get back up again."

Emily looked toward heaven. "We'll help you up, you ninny. No, not now. Stand up. Let me tell you the rest."

She and Iris pulled on Amanda's arms and hoisted her back up off her knees. Emily had it all worked out and a few minutes later they put the plan into action.

Amanda pretended to try to climb up on the chair to look out the high window. "I'm going to see if I can see out this high window," she said loudly. Then she screamed and lay down on the floor as the others shouted, "Amanda! Watch out! Oh, no!" and stomped their feet. Mona knocked the chair on its side. They all knelt around Amanda shouting things like, "Amanda? Are you okay?" and, "You idiot! What were you thinking?" That was Mona.

Amanda wailed. "My hip, my hip!"

Iris flew to the door, screaming, "Help!" She pounded, then pulled, tugged and rattled the doorknob. "Help!" She tried for all the pathos and fear she could put into the one word and was rewarded by the sound of hurrying feet and curses outside. Then the lock turned and the door opened a crack. One of the men peered in.

"What's going on?"

Iris shouted in his face. "My friend has injured herself. I think she's broken her hip. This is dreadful."

The man pushed the door open further and looked into the room. Amanda continued to wail and hammer her fists on the floor.

"We can't lift her," said Emily. Iris could tell Emily was trying to make her face look as pathetic as possible. Which wasn't very pathetic, she wasn't good at it. "Every time we try to move her, she moans so bad."

"She's in a lot of pain," said Mona, looking from the man back down to Amanda. "There, there, sweetheart." She patted Amanda's hand. Iris couldn't help smiling at the dramatics. Her play-acting friend Sam would love this.

The man shut the door. Iris frowned, wondering if he'd locked himself in with them, which would be of little help. Iris saw Mona's eyes gleam as the man stepped toward the group around the woman on the floor. Behind him, she signaled to her sister to be patient. They had to get the other man in here, too.

"Don't touch me!" Amanda wailed even more. There were tears trickling down her cheeks. Where had this sudden acting ability come from? Maybe Amanda really was in pain lying there on the hard floor. She had been through a lot today.

Emily looked up at the man, and in her team leader voice, commanded, "She needs help, badly. You're going to have to call an ambulance."

The man jerked and his face went white. "No, we can't do that. I'll help you get her up on the bed."

"Mona has several fused disks," said Iris, shaking her head. "She can't help or we'll have two screaming patients."

Mona stepped back and Iris, Emily and the man stood around Amanda. She continued to shout the house down in pain and fear. It was quite harrowing, and Iris, who was directly opposite the man, tried not to grin. They followed his directions and reached down.

"Be careful, Iris," said Mona, wringing her hands. "For god's sake, you're almost eighty."

"She's right," said Iris, trying to squat far enough to reach Amanda. She put a pained expression on her face and clutched at her low back. "I can't do it. I'm sorry, Amanda."

"Uh," said the man. "I'll go get my . . . buddy." There was something odd about the guy's voice. It cracked like he was just going through puberty. He walked to the door. Behind his back Iris signaled to the group to keep it up. Amanda moaned. Emily soothed her. Mona and Iris clung to each other and wept loudly.

It took a few moments, but sure enough, the other man came in, closed and locked the door behind him. He took stock of the scene and nodded to his friend.

"You lot back up," he said gruffly, glaring at them. Emily stepped away and the two men flanked Amanda. As they squatted down and put their hands under her, the three friends pounced. Mona knocked one man sideways by swinging the chair at him and catching him in the shoulder. The other said, "What the . . .," straightened up, and took a step toward Emily. Iris grabbed his wrist and executed her patented hip throw. He landed on his back with a loud "O☐ of," and then a moan.

"Wow!" said Emily, eyes wide. "That was awesome. I need you to teach me that." Then she and Iris piled on top of the man, who was now kicking and yelling. Though they were small, they were committed, and soon they had him subdued. Amanda rolled over and laid on top of the one Mona had coshed. Iris grabbed Mona's new scarf off the bed and knotted it around her victim's hands. Emily sat on his kicking legs while Iris took the string that had bound her wrists out of her pocket and transferred it to his feet. When her victim was trussed, she crawled over and went to work on the one Mona and Amanda were sitting on.

Breathing hard, Iris struggled back to her feet and looked around. Amanda and Mona were sitting next to their kidnapper now. He appeared to be just waking up from sleep. Emily was on her feet, but bending over the kidnapper she and Iris had taken down, peering at his face. He was glaring back and yelling something about this not being what it looked like. Which was weird. Then Emily reached out with one hand and yanked at the guy's face. He emitted a high-pitched scream of pain and thrashed around even more. With the other hand, Emily knocked off his hat.

Iris started to laugh. She'd seen a transformation like this in Amsterdam. This time, looking up at them from the floor was a woman with short blond hair, and the fake mustache dangled from Emily's fingers.

Emily laughed too, and patted the fake hair back into place, crooked. Then she righted the battered chair and slid it over to where Mona and Amanda could lean on it while she helped them get to their feet.

"Whew," said Amanda. "That's more work than I've done in years. And it felt great!"

Mona said nothing, but she looked even paler than before.

"You need to go lie down again, Mona."

"I will," she said weakly, "before Iris makes me. That was frigging impressive, Sis."

"Thank you, Mona." Iris felt warm with accomplishment and pride.

"Now," said Emily. "Let's look at what we have here." She bent and stripped the fake mustache off the other guy.

The four of them looked down at their captives. Rather than the men they thought they were catching, two small women gazed up at them from the floor, looking wary and belligerent. They were almost identical, down to the fake mustaches. The only difference was their hair. Now that their caps had fallen off, Iris saw one had dark, shoulder-length hair pulled up in a messy topknot. The other wore hers in short blond spikes.

"You must be sisters," said Amanda. "You look alike."

"Why are you disguised as men?" asked Mona, holding her head and swaying.

"Are you okay?" asked the blond woman, staring up at Mona wide eyed.

"Oh, now you're concerned about me? What about back there in the woods when you tackled me and threw me in your van?"

"I'm really sorry we had to do . . ." the blond began.

"It's a long story," said the dark one.

"We've got nowhere more interesting to be at the moment," said Iris, moving to Mona's side and supporting her weight.

The blond sighed. "The short version is, our family's most prized heirloom has been taken and we have to come up with the money to buy her back. So we took on a second job."

Mona looked at Iris, Iris looked at Amanda, and Amanda looked at Emily, who just shook her head.

Iris turned back to the woman. "I think we're going to need the long version."

"A job," said Mona, "as kidnappers?"

"We're not kidnappers," said the two in unison, shaking their heads.

"A moment ago you said an heirloom was stolen. Then you called it her. Why do you call an heirloom her?" asked Amanda.

The dark haired one sighed. "It's a painting by Vermeer. Of one of our ancestors."

The four friends all gasped.

Emily sat back as if slapped. "Well, it's so comforting to have been kidnapped by cultured crooks."

"Your family had their portraits painted by Vermeer?" Amanda could hardly get the words out past the awe in her voice.

"No, not the way you think." The dark-haired sister shook her head. "Our family has never been wealthy. But they had this one beautiful thing, a small painting of a great-great-grandma. Her name was Femke. Family legend has it that she was a maid in Vermeer's house."

"Like the girl with the pearl earring?" Amanda visibly swooned with artistic rapture. Iris reached out and caught her arm, too. The blond nodded and took up the story again.

"Right. It was a homey scene of a young woman sewing beside the fire. Sort of like the girl with a pearl earring. Except this one was of our great-great-great – whole bunch of greats – grandmother. She was just a girl. You can imagine. What with Vermeer's reputation."

"Oh, my," said Amanda. "Yes."

The blond picked up the story where he sister left off. "It was protected by our family for generations. They were part of the resistance during the war. They smuggled it across borders, hid it from Nazis, the whole gamut."

"So where is it now?" asked Emily. "You said it was stolen."

"Yes. We let it get away." The brunette said, with a catch in her voice.

"One of us," the blond went on, her eyes cast down. "I won't say which, got involved with a good-looking man. She let him into our home. She slept with him, she fell in love with him. When he admired the painting of Great-Great-Great-Grandmother Femke, one of us told him about the painting and how important it's been to our family."

"And now it . . . she . . . is being held for ransom," the brunette went on, wiping a tear from her cheek. "It was me. I've let down generations of grandparents, aunts, uncles and cousins who protected the portrait through fire, famine, plague, wars, religious persecution, societal collapse. And I let it get taken out of our comfortable, middle-class living room. The irony makes me weep."

"So we need $200,000 dollars to buy it back," said the blond.

"Cripes," said Emily. "That's a lot of money."

"We've been earning it little by little. Only ninety-five thousand to go." The brunette sister turned a fake grin on her blond sibling.

"You earn it by ransoming people?" asked Amanda. "You got the wrong girls this time. We don't have any money for you."

Iris felt Mona sway against her and looked up. Mona's face was drained of color. Iris put her arm around her sister's shoulders in case she fainted.

"We already got the money back that you stole," said the blond. "We don't kidnap people."

"You said that before, but here we are. You grabbed us off the side of the road and you locked us in here. That's a lot like kidnapping, if you ask me," said Emily.

"We just needed to hold you for a little while. Gloria Trammel, the woman whose bag you stole, wants us to find out who you're working for and what you planned to do with her bag," said the brunette. "Are you working with the police or on your own?"

Mona, Amanda, and Emily all looked at Iris. "Aha," said Emily.

Iris held up her hands. "Whoa, whoa, whoa. You have the wrong idea. We're not working with anyone. We never intended to steal your bag. I just thought it was mine." She grinned. "I'd misplaced it. They're almost the same color. Just an innocent mistake."

"Which has caused us a whole lot of grief," said Mona. "I have to sit down." She shuffled in the direction of the bed. Iris helped her lower herself to the edge.

Guilt dug its claws into Iris' throat. "I'm sorry, Mona. I know this has been hard on you. When I saw you running across the parking lot I worried you would overdo it."

Mona let out a short laugh. "Running. Is that what you call that stiff-hipped shuffle I do when I try to hurry?"

"Hold on," said Amanda, with more command than was customary for her. "I want the whole story. Start from the beginning. Why was all that money in Mrs. Trammel's bag, the bag that Iris stole . . . by accident? And why did she send you to get it back from us? Why didn't she call the police or casino security? And while we're at it, I'm with Mona – you need to explain why you're disguised as men. You could earn money for a ransom just as well looking like yourselves." The tone in her voice reminded Iris that this woman had spent years and years turning wayward teenagers into professional artists.

"We thought it would be best if we didn't look like ourselves when we're engaged in criminal acts." said the blond.

Mona moaned and lay down. "I can't . . ." She whispered. "I have . . ." she paused and breathed rapidly. "Carrie."

Iris held Mona's hand while she listened to the story.

The blond sister gave them a sad smile. "My name is Sunshine. I work for Mrs. Trammel, the gambling commissioner's wife. As her personal assistant. I handle all the books and accounts for her business. I figured out a while ago that in addition to her beauty and fashion work, Gloria had quite a lucrative grift in place. When the painting was stolen and we needed so much more money, I was sad, and overwhelmed and frightened. And in a momentary lapse of reason, I helped myself to a little here, a little there. Now I'm stuck assisting with the con." She brightened slightly. "I've done all right, though, so it looks like she'll let me keep my main job."

"Sunshine got caught taking a few thousand out of the funds Gloria got off her victims."

"I was desperate. I thought she wouldn't notice. I didn't know she had a camera on me. I should have assumed she would. It's obvious when I think about it now. So she confronted me with my crime, and she made me her bitch."

"Gloria is punishing her by making us both do her dirty work."

Mona turned and opened her eyes. "So, what's your name? And how did you get involved?" she asked the brunette.

"I'm Helen. I'm a freelance floral designer, which means I'm broke half the time. During one of my dry spells, Sun talked Gloria into having me do the floral work for one of her soirees. Ever since, Gloria has always held that over her as a big favor she'd done us. When Sun got caught, she gave me a choice. Either she would turn Sun over to the cops or we could team up to help her. She knew money would motivate us. So now we transport the money she gets from casinos for her and we get a cut."

"What's the sun got to do with it?" asked Iris.

"I'm not sure what you mean," said Helen, blinking.

The blond laughed. "Sun is short for Sunshine. It's my nickname."

"I'm Iris," said Iris pointing to herself. "This is Emily, and Amanda. Mona is there on the bed, she's my sister."

"Why does this Trammel woman want to steal from the casino?" asked Amanda. "Does she hate the tribe?"

"It looked like she was their darling this morning," said Mona.

"Crooks don't have to have something against Native Americans to steal from them," said Emily.

"That would be racist," said Amanda. "You have to report her."

Sunshine smiled ruefully. "If only. We can't report her for that or anything else. She's got evidence that I stole money from her. She'd use that against us."

"She's connected," said Helen.

"And she has deep pockets," said Sunshine. "She would win."

"Hold on," Mona's voice was weak, but still commanding. We're getting all confused here," said Mona. "Back up a bit. What was it again that got you on the bad side of that bitch? Just stealing a few dollars?"

"Yeah, more than a few. Like I said, I figured out that she's running this grift. And I knew where she kept a lot of cash, and I liberated enough that she eventually noticed."

"Oh. Okay, go on."

"She doesn't have anything against the tribe. We're not sure exactly what her actual game is. But here at Blackfish, she seems to be targeting a woman in the auditing department."

"Maybe she slept with her husband or something," said Emily, with a leer.

"Maybe. She's making it look like that woman embezzled the money. I don't know exactly how. She gets a bag full of cash every few days. Our part is disabling the security system while they make the exchange. Then she puts her bag somewhere out of the range of cameras and we take the money away."

"Today was a little different," said Helen. "I think she's upping the ante. She had us put the woman's finger prints on a gun."

"Aha!" Emily jumped up and down. "I saw you," she said, pointing at one, then the other. "I saw one of you." She turned a gloating smile on her friends. "I told you it wasn't a bill folder. I was right."

The sisters looked at one another. "I guess we shouldn't be surprised. We do this so often we've gotten a little lax."

"You do this often? The blackmail?" said Amanda.

"Yes," said Sunshine. "Every few weeks we come up here and go through this routine. She gets the money, we pretend to fix shit, we pick up the cash and we scram."

Helen continued the story. "Today she left her bag on the table outside the conference room for us. We were to transfer the money to our satchel and take it to the van."

"We go all over the state with her doing variations of this same routine," added Sunshine. "She puts on an event at a casino, Helen does the flowers. We integrate ourselves with the staff. Gloria's constantly working the angles, trying to arrange another victim."

Helen shook her head, dejected. "It's the worst. We wear uniforms of one kind or another and look busy in various casinos, like we belong there, fixing things, delivering things, while Gloria wines and dines. We're always decked out with clipboards or laptop cases. While she distracts everyone with gift bags, or tales of her husband's latest arrest, or planned fee hikes or whatever, we slip in and make the transfer."

"She tells a good story," said Sunshine to her sister. "You have to give her that. Keeps the workers spellbound so we always get away clean."

"Now I'm confused," said Emily. "Back up a step. Her husband got arrested? More than once?"

"What?" said Sunshine.

The dark sister laughed. "No, her husband is Bill Trammel. Director of the state gaming commission. He sometimes has people arrested when they mess with the rules of gambling."

"Ahhh."

The blond, Sunshine, continued the story. "She goes to all the casinos in a certain area, about once every couple of weeks. She says she likes casinos, likes to stay current on what her love is doing. But her goal is to extract money from each. I don't know what she actually does to get this money – we're not in on that part of her scheme. But she sure doesn't want anyone to see her with it."

"Does she do it by gaming?" said Emily. "Is she a card sharp?"

Helen shook her head. "I don't think that can be it. She'd be in violation of all kinds of regulations and under too much scrutiny."

"She's not open about her grift," said Sunshine, "and I've never found any kind of record in her office."

"I've always assumed it's blackmail," said Helen. "Not something criminals tend to keep track of."

"Now that we're involved, I keep track of it," said Sunshine. "However she gets it, we always take the money away for her, so I have a record of what we've transported and from where."

"But we've failed," said Helen. "Here we are, you lot figured us out."

Her blond sister smiled at her. "You know, Helen, we're actually terrible at this. I spend all my time crying. You can't sleep."

"Then why do it?" said Iris. "There must be another way to get your painting back."

"Look at us. We're not exactly Seal Team Six." Sunshine indicated their small stature. "We're reasonably fit, but we're five foot two. There's no way we're going to get our property back by throwing our weight around."

"My dear," said Iris, in her most commanding voice, sitting up very straight, "don't sell yourselves short. Stature is no indication of skill. I am five foot one and I've recently learned that I can do just about anything I put my mind to. You've got an inch on me, and about fifty years. Plus there are two of you. So I'm not listening to excuses. You have what it takes. You just have to get brave, get busy, get that terrible woman and get your painting back."

Five pairs of shocked eyes stared up at Iris. Five mouths gaped. Even Mona, who had turned to watch the conversation, forgot to keep her face immobile. Iris noticed her sister was breathing strangely again. She sounded like Amanda when she needed her inhaler.

Helen, recovered first and fidgeted, jerking her bound hands up and down. "I enjoyed that rousing speech and all. But I'm sitting here, feet and hands bound. And I'm not trying to be disrespectful, but I was just taken down by a gang of women who can't lift their hands over their heads. I'm not feeling the sense of empowerment you seem to think I should."

"Yeah," said Sunshine, "this is not our finest hour."

"You'll have better days," said Amanda, beginning to nod her head. "We're not seals either. Some days it's all I can do to get out of bed. We're more like squirrels. But I bet we could take down more crooks if we wanted. Not that we think you're crooks." She blushed and everyone hooted. "I'm not kidding though. We've got some skills."

"She's right about one thing," said Emily. "All these skills we've amassed over our long lives are only good if we remember to use them enough that they don't get rusty. What better way to sharpen up than by launching a night-time ninja attack on Jack's house, to steal a priceless painting back? We'll call ourselves Squirrel Team Six. Who wants to be in charge of getting the t-shirts printed?" They all started laughing.

"All kidding aside," said Iris, between giggles. "These girls need their painting back so they can get out from under the thumb of that gold-digging menace. We need to help them. Emily,

Amanda, Mona, we can do this. We may be squirrels, but even squirrels have a plan."

CHAPTER 10

While Emily wrangled the full story of the man who'd stolen the painting out of Sunshine and Helen, Iris sat down beside Mona and took her hand.

"I think we need to get you to a doctor."

Mona shook her head. "You think I haven't been to the doctor? Have you forgotten who you're talking to? I've been. Believe me, I've been to so many doctors about this. I know what to expect and I've accepted what's coming. My body is shutting down, little by little. I feel bad for a while, and then I rally."

Iris looked into Mona's eyes for a moment. "I'm not convinced, but sleep for a bit while I sort out what we're going to do next. It's all well and good to talk about getting even with Gloria Trammel, but at least two of us are still prisoners." Iris patted her sister's hand, and pulled the blanket over her shoulders. Mona nodded and shut her eyes.

"We should untie them," said Amanda as Iris rejoined the others.

"I think we'll leave that until we've got more information," said Emily. "I'm still skeptical of this stolen painting story. It's just too fantastic. Vermeer." She snorted, pulled the chair over, sat down and crossed her arms like a judge.

The wrangling in low voices went on for a few minutes. They tossed ideas back and forth, then Mona called Iris over.

"What do you need?"

"Sis, I've been listening to these plans and it's just too much. Those two are nice girls, and you, Amanda, and Emily are nice. And not only nice, but old to boot. Your antiquated skills are not going to be a match for a strong young man with technology. That's not a recipe for going crashing into some man's house to steal a painting."

"I know it sounds difficult, but . . ."

"It sounds insane," said Mona. "I've got another solution."

Iris sat down. "Okay, I'm all ears."

"I won a jackpot. My bag is in your car, tucked up under my seat. It has $150,000 in it."

"What?!" Iris shouted, jumping to her feet.

"Shhh."

Iris looked at the others. They were staring at her. She smiled, got control of herself, sat back down on the bed and spoke softly. "That's amazing. How did that happen? When did that happen? Was that you yelling? Wait. You've been wandering around with $150,000 dollars in your purse? Are you crazy? They could have sent it to you bit by bit. Plus, then you'd get more. Why did you take the one-time cash payout? You are crazy."

"Iris, I'm dying."

"You're not dying, Mona." Iris felt fierce. "I admit, you've been looking weak and acting strangely. We just need to get you to a hospital for some tests."

"Would you shut up and listen to me?" said Mona, gripping Iris' forearm. "I've been to the hospital. I've had all the tests. I've got all this money that I don't need. You don't need it. Carrie doesn't need it or want it. Rumor has it I can't take it with me. So I want to put it somewhere it can do some good. I want to give that money to Sunshine and Helen. Then they'll have enough to buy their Grandmother Femke painting back and stop doing that bitch's dirty work and expose her crimes without fear. Maybe they can even go to the cops and get that criminal boyfriend put in jail, too."

Iris couldn't stop shaking her head. Her throat had closed completely. She struggled to speak. "I . . . I don't even know who I'm talking to. Your brain isn't working normally. You've never cared about people doing bad things to each other. You like hospitals." She patted Mona's hand. "I know, I'll take you to University, they're the best. After a few days under a handsome doctor's care you'll feel better. I'll get the keys to the van." She began to rise, but Mona's grip on her forearm was like grim death.

"Stop it, Iris. I can tell the end is coming. I used the last of my energy for that little show we put on to get out of the casino. The van ride was the last straw. And then I pushed past the end to help you capture these two. Now I can hardly move. My head is splitting apart. My vision is about gone. If I go to a hospital, I'll die there. I'd rather die as part of Squirrel Team Six." She smiled. Plus, without me you'd be five and that's just not right. I can at least stick around to correct you when you start to do something stupid."

Iris grimaced. "See, just talking about doctors is helping already. Now you sound like yourself." She shook her head. "But I doubt that woman will let Helen and Sunshine go, even if they use your money to buy the painting back. What if she presses charges?"

"That's the job you and the squirrel team need to do. Help them get the dirt on Trammel so they can expose her. And afterward, if I'm not around to do it, give them my winnings." Mona released Iris' arm and closed her eyes again.

Iris watched her breathing slow, then sat listening to the discussion. But she didn't really hear what the others were saying. She was boggled by the changes in Mona. Her sister had always been selfish, self-centered, self-important. All the worst self words fit Mona.

She'd also always liked to be sick or injured, she liked going to the doctor in a way that creeped Iris out. From their phone conversations over the years, Iris had divined that being in a small room with all attention focused on her gave Mona some kind of validation. Being an invalid, in some strange way, increased her sense of worth. She remembered her sister saying things like, "The young doctor was very handsome. He got his degree from John's Hopkins and he spent a long time with me checking out all my symptoms. He thought my case was one of the most interesting he'd ever seen." The craving to have a good-looking, impeccably credentialed, young doctor fawning over her was so pronounced that Iris was convinced Mona had made up many of her injuries and conditions over the years. Now, here she was looking and acting really sick and she didn't want to go to the hospital. What had come over her?

Iris looked down at Mona's sleeping form. Her sister looked thin and shrunken. Her body hardly made a ridge under the blanket. Maybe Mona really was dying. It sure seemed like she'd given up. Usually she was acquisitive. This desire to give something away, let alone $150,000, certainly was a sign of some kind of change in her life.

Mona had noticed changes in Iris, too. It had been nice to hear her surprised at things Iris had done, when all their lives Mona had only been disappointed in her. She'd especially hated the way Iris did everything their mother demanded. Now she'd seen that little sister had more fire in her than before, and Iris liked seeing a touch of respect from her.

"Right, Iris?"

Iris jumped, and her eyes focused. Four women were looking at her. Three from the floor. She'd been sitting here staring at them. They must have the mistaken impression that she'd been listening.

"What? I'm afraid I didn't hear . . ."

"I told you she wasn't listening," said Emily crossly.

"Do you have something on your mind, dear?" asked Amanda.

Iris snorted softly. "Just a few things." Making sure not to jostle the bed, she got up and walked over to join them. She dropped her voice. "Let's talk softer so that Mona can rest. Now what am I agreeing to this time?"

"I just said you weren't afraid to take on thugs bigger than these two. From what you said about Amsterdam and all," said Emily.

"And I told them you're a great driver," said Amanda.

"Yes, that's why my car is currently engulfed in forest."

"We all make mistakes now and then," said Amanda. "Did you see the way the light fell through the leaves? There were a thousand shades of green in that forest."

Iris shook her head at her friend and directed the conversation back on track. "What does my driving have to do with anything?"

"We're thinking you should drive the getaway car," said Sunshine.

Iris jerked to attention. "What getaway car?"

"When we steal the painting back from Jack," said Helen.

"Who is Jack?"

Emily sighed. "Boy, you really haven't been listening. We've been talking about him for half an hour. Jack is Helen's ex-boyfriend. The one who is holding the painting for ransom."

"Not a very nice guy, by the way," said Amanda to the dark-haired sister. "I'm sorry to say this, but you have an unfortunate taste in men."

"Clearly she takes after Grandmother Femke," said Sunshine.

"We're planning how to help them get the painting back from that thief," said Emily.

"Oh, okay. Sure." Iris envisioned herself and her friends wearing black ninja garb and tiptoeing through dark rooms. She started when she realized Mona was not in her imagined scene. She looked across the room and saw Mona looking at her with the tiniest of smiles on her thin lips.

While the group quietly ran some more ideas past her. Iris mulled over what Mona had said. She nodded at most of the suggestions, gasped at a few, but her mind was still on Mona and her surprising proposal. Finally, she kneeled beside Sunshine and whispered in the girl's ear. Sunshine jumped, looked at her wide eyed. Then looked to Mona, mouth hanging open. Iris patted her knee and struggled back to her feet. She went back across the room, sat on the edge of the bed again and took Mona's hand. "I love you, Sis. I'm sorry for yelling at you earlier."

There was a fluttering pressure of Mona's fingers on Iris' palm in response, but her eyes closed again.

Iris' throat closed. She couldn't breathe. Her eyes stung.

Mona's eyes opened again. "One more thing, Iris." Her voice was a whisper.

Iris leaned closer and whispered back. "Yes?"

"I've been hard on you. All your life." Her words came slowly, with her breath. "I've been hard on everybody. It's not that I don't love you . . ." Her voice trailed away.

"It's okay, Mona," Iris said quietly, patting her sister's hand. "Water under the bridge at this point."

"It is." Mona's nod was almost imperceptible. "But I still want to say this. I'm proud. Of you. You've done amazing things. Today."

"Thank you, Mona. I appreciate hearing that." Iris dashed a tear from her eye, ignoring the idea that she'd just heard one last backhanded compliment. "You've done some pretty great things today yourself." She wiped a tear from her other eye. "We could have made a great team, if we'd tried."

Mona smiled. "You're right about that, too. And we may still have a little time for teamwork. I may rally yet. I'm sorry. I'm not going to be strong enough to . . ." She stopped and closed her eyes, pain evident in the lines of her face, " . . .to help boost you in through a window or something." She chuckled softly, then swallowed and closed her eyes. "But let me rest a bit. And if you choose to go through with this cockamamie scheme . . . I'd be honored to drive the getaway car."

Iris wiped away tears as she started to laugh, but a harsh voice cut her off.

"Well, Helen, Sunshine, it looks like I got here just in time."

Gasping, they all spun toward the sound of the voice. In the doorway stood the woman in pink. Iris jumped to her feet, trying to shield Mona from the intruder.

Lipstick glossy red, not a hair out of place, Gloria Trammel stood there, surveying each of them where they sat and lay. While they all looked beat up, tangle-haired and half dead, she looked as flawless as ever. Her diamond earrings glinted as she turned her head. Elegant, polished, and smiling, the perfect society wife arriving at a soiree. Except for the gun she was pointing at them.

CHAPTER 11

"Gloria," said Sunshine. Her voice was pitched as welcoming, but judging from the look on her face, Iris didn't think she was really that happy to see the Chanel-clad woman.

"Get back, you two." The elegant woman waved the gun at Emily and Amanda. Emily rose from the chair and took a step back. Amanda, who was sitting on the floor with the sisters, struggled to her feet and joined her friend.

Trammel shook her head, then smiled sweetly at her two helpers where they sat, still tied, on the floor, then gave a Vaudeville villain's laugh. "I certainly never expected to have to rescue you from a band of dotty little old ladies."

"They turned out to have some pretty good tricks," said Sunshine. "They surprised us." Helen chewed her lip.

"Lucky for you I decided to come check on my money then, isn't it?"

"Yes," said Helen. "Very lucky." Iris noticed that her voice had taken on a guttural quality. As if speaking to this woman made her want to vomit.

"You won't get away with this," said Iris, because somebody had to. Behind her she heard Mona's soft snicker, and her heart warmed that after all they'd been through, they'd reconnected enough to share a joke. She turned and smiled at her sister.

"Oh, I'm doing fine. You're the ones who won't get away." Their captor turned her haughty gaze on Iris. She tilted her head, then waved the gun at Iris. "You, shorty, come here. The rest of you stay where you are."

Iris frowned and stayed where she was. "My sister is ill. We need to get her . . ."

"Now," said Trammel. Her eyes never left Iris' as she slowly, theatrically, raised the gun until it was pointing steadily at Mona. If there had been a red target dot in the center of Mona's forehead, the message could not have been clearer.

Gulping back the tears that sprang to her eyes, Iris forced herself to walk to the vile woman's side.

"That's better," said Trammel. She reached out and grabbed Iris' arm and jerked her into a one-armed bear hug, the gun jammed against her temple.

"Iris," the word was only a whisper.

Iris tried to see Mona, but Trammel prevented her. No matter how she struggled the woman blocked the view. Gloria Trammel was stronger than her trophy-wife exterior would lead one to believe.

"I am not pleased to have to do this, Sunshine. You and your sister were to take care of everything for me. If I have to handle it myself, I'm certainly not going to pay you."

"We'll handle it all, Gloria, no problem." Sunshine gulped. "Though we will need you to untie us."

"You, Mrs. Bear Grylls," Trammel said to Emily, "you look like you've got enough brains to be able to deal with a knot. Untie them. No tricks. Be aware, this hostage is expendable."

Her eyes glued to the gun at Iris' head, Emily did as she was told. The sisters jumped to their feet, massaging their wrists. Then Sunshine grabbed Emily and pinned her arms behind her. Helen jumped slightly as she watched her sister, but then followed suit, wrestling a squawking Amanda into submission.

"Good. I'm taking this one as my hostage. Lock the rest of them in. You will transport the money now. I'm going to follow you to make sure nothing goes wrong this time."

Helen balked. "Gloria, we can't leave them all here. If something happens to them . . . This is our home. The cops . . ."

"Do I look like I care what the police think about you? You're already a criminal. Your sister stole from me and you were complicit. And you've been transporting money stolen from casinos. Your van is on every security camera in the state casino system." She paused, and smiled. "We registered it in your name, remember? I can just turn you in now, if you prefer."

Helen looked at Sunshine, but didn't say anything more.

Trammel shoved Iris in front of her toward the door. "I thought not." Iris tripped over her own feet, trying to match her steps to the younger woman's long stride. The sisters fell in behind them.

Pushing her neck to its limit, Iris was just able to glimpse Mona watching her and struggling to sit up in the bed. Then she coughed and fell back.

"Mona," said Iris. Her sister raised a weak hand and blew her a kiss. Iris' tears let loose as she was propelled out of the room.

"Please. My sister is very ill. I need to be with her."

"Oh, it is so very sad." Trammel said as she marched Iris down the hall. "But you're going to have to get over it."

"Load the money in the van," she said to the sisters as she pushed Iris into the kitchen. "We're taking it now."

"All of it? All at once?" Sunshine looked incredulous.

"Yes. We have to get all evidence out of here and deal with these troublesome old women. Did you find out who they are working for?"

"They said it was only a case of mistaken identity," said Helen.

"Yes, it was just me," sobbed Iris. "The others didn't do anything. I thought your bag was mine. They're the same color. Please, call an ambulance. My sister is dying."

"Everybody dies. Fact of life. Besides, if you're like all the other sisters I know, you actually hate each other, you just won't admit it."

"What does the quality of our relationship have to do with taking care of a human life? There are many people I have no relationship with whatsoever. And a few I wish I'd never met. That doesn't mean I want to see harm come to them. How can you be so callous?"

"Shut up," said Trammel, jabbing Iris in the neck with the gun. "Sit." She pushed Iris down into a chair at the kitchen table and resumed speaking to the sisters.

"Clean out the van to remove any trace of these old goof-balls – hair, crumpled tissues, hearing aids, false teeth, whatever. Then load the money in, and make sure to bury the boxes under some of the ones full of books, kitchen goods, etcetera, in case you're stopped. And change out of those stupid uniforms. You're just a couple of sisters moving to a new apartment. My boxes are already marked, right?"

"All but the money from today," said Sunshine.

"That was my next question. You recovered my purse from this idiot?"

"Yes," Sunshine pointed to the table where a cloth-covered lump lay.

"A bath towel?" The look of disgust on Trammel's face made both sisters cringe. "Impressive security measures. Good thing none of your nosy neighbors dropped in this time." She waved the gun at the younger women. "Get on with it."

The two sisters glanced at each other, then left the room. A moment later Iris heard scrapes, bumps and the sound of a door closing coming from down the hall.

Trammel inspected an armchair, then carefully sat in it, crossing her long, tanned legs and training the gun on Iris. "Not a word," she said. She laid the gun on her thigh, business end still pointed at Iris, took out her phone and began texting.

Iris strained to hear her friends in the bedroom, but there was no sound. She'd expected Emily to set up a ruckus right away. She hoped they were alright. And Mona . . . she had to try one more time to convince the woman to help her.

"My sister desperately needs a doctor." She blurted the words as loud and as fast as she could. "Please."

Trammel paused her thumb typing and looked at Iris with narrowed eyes. Then her glossy red lips turned up in a snarky smile. "What your sister needs," she said slowly, "is to die, and get out of my way. Now resume your silence, because if you say another word I'll be happy to hasten the process."

Iris choked back the next words and clenched her fists, trying to stop shaking with fear and rage. She'd been ready to get shot herself – though it seemed a pretty harsh penalty for simply talking too much, but she couldn't put anyone else's life in danger.

The two sisters came back into the room. They'd changed into everyday clothes – jeans, t-shirts, and tennis shoes. Sunshine wore a ball cap that all but covered her short hair. Helen had hers wrapped in a bandanna.

"Ready to go," said Sunshine.

Trammel nodded, then turned to Iris and indicated with the gun that she should stand. "Bathroom." She grinned. "I have a

109

Grandma. I know what happens as soon as we pull out of the driveway."

Iris got to her feet and slowly straightened her stiff back, groaning slightly. If she were going to be a grandma, then by god she would be the most grandma-y grandma ever. "Oooh, my back. Just give me a minute. I've been sitting in that hard chair a long time."

Trammel rolled her eyes, but didn't hurry her.

When Iris had stretched thoroughly, Trammel led her to the bathroom. Iris dawdled, wishing she could pull off another bathroom escape like she'd engineered in Ireland. But unlike Hal Smith, the gentlemanly smuggler who had captured Iris at the Giant's Causeway, Gloria Trammel had no compunction about leaving the door open while Iris did her business. Which made it a very uncomfortable business indeed.

Next, Trammel directed her to the kitchen door, but spoke to the sisters. "We'll go around the side. We'll be less likely to be noticed than if we went out the front door."

Trammel jabbed Iris in the back with the gun propelling her through the backyard. The fruit trees, Iris noted, could use a good pruning, but the garden and lawn were reasonably neat. She wondered if Emily and Amanda were watching them from the window of their prison.

Trammel opened the gate while tucking the gun into the waistband of her skirt. Iris laughed inside. If only Mona could see the use her coveted Chanel suit was being put to.

The woman grasped Iris' arm. "Here, let me help you, Grandma. You're going to continue doing what I say. The gun can be back on you in a second, and your sister and friends will live or die based on the way you behave." She smiled indulgently. For those nosy neighbors who might be watching, Iris assumed.

In the driveway sat the beautiful gold car. As they approached, the door changed shape and Iris jumped. A door handle had rotated out from the edge. "I'll let you drive," said Trammel with a snide smile. "It'll be such a treat for you."

Iris faltered, but she put her hand under the newly sprouted handle. The door opened without her having to pull. Surprised, she hesitated again, then saw Trammel's serial killer eyes boring into her and lowered herself into the driver's seat. Trammel "helped" her, then closed the door and went around to the opposite side, getting in just as the garage door slid up.

Iris looked around for the ignition, but before she could even ask for the key, the dash lights came on.

"Go ahead," said Trammel, a huge smile still on her face as if she were really enjoying this, and the gun in her hand again. "Back out."

"But the motor isn't running," Iris bent sideways to look for the ignition. "Where are the keys?"

Suddenly the car began rolling backward. Iris yelped, grabbed the wheel and stomped around looking for the brake. The car kept rolling, as she struggled to turn and look over her shoulder.

"Relax, Iris. May I call you Iris?"

"You're the one with the gun."

The car stopped in the street. When the van backed out of the driveway, the car inched backward, giving the larger vehicle space. The garage door rolled back down.

"Follow," said Trammel.

"Aaahh," said Iris, as the car silently started forward. She gripped the wheel and steered as they came to the corner.

With Iris hyperventilating, cringing, and flinging the wheel back and forth, the car made the turn following the van. It seemed to be keeping a safe distance.

Trammel was leaning back against the passenger door, watching her struggles and laughing.

"This is some car," said Iris, trying to loosen her grip as the wheel turned one way, then the other. "It . . . I can't . . . good lord . . .. Do I need to do anything?"

"No. All your silly efforts, though highly entertaining, are a waste of time. The car doesn't care what you do." She took out a pink phone. "This will make a great video. A warning to all my young fans to take care of themselves better than you did." She laughed as they rounded another bend. "Flail and shriek all you want. It's in driver-less mode. You can hold the wheel if you like, but you are just a passenger, unless you press the mode button and select manual drive. Which you will not."

When the car reached a straight section of road and she could stop flinching at each turn, Iris resumed breathing and looked around at the controls. She didn't see a mode button anywhere. Just a lit up screen, sort of like her tablet and her phone.

A moment later, the car was following the van up a ramp and Iris completely freaked out. She couldn't control her shrieking as the vehicle sped up to an ungodly velocity. Her head snapped back, her innards felt squeezed, her lungs wouldn't take in air. The car merged onto the freeway into a space Iris would never have tried to squeeze her little Honda into. The sensation was eerie and disconcerting, beyond just the potential collisions. Iris couldn't figure out why the experience felt so odd until the car settled into traffic beside a big pickup truck with a noisy engine and she realized that the whole sequence had taken place silently. There was no engine sound.

She clenched her hands harder on the wheel in an effort to steady her racing heart and stop her nerves bouncing all over her body.

Then she noticed that, beside her, Gloria Trammel was laughing. She actually found Iris' fear funny.

Iris' blood boiled. This bitch was going down if it was the last thing Iris did with her sorry life.

Fighting for control of her emotions, Iris yelped once more as the car changed lanes, then smiled into Trammel's phone. "This is so . . . different." Her arms were aching with tension. She didn't think she could unclench her fingers. There were probably finger indentations in the wheel.

"It does take a little getting used to." Trammel's gun hand lay relaxed in her lap now. But the gun was once again pointed at Iris' middle.

"What kind is it? My friend thought it was a Tesla, but they have a T on the back. I didn't see a T there, and I don't see any logos in here."

"It's a prototype. My ex-husband is an executive in automotive design. I'm not at liberty to discuss what make this is. I'm on the books as a beta tester, that way he can always supply me with the latest model before anyone else has it."

The way she said it, the officious and self-important tone, Iris could tell Trammel considered herself the one in control of the arrangement. That must have been some divorce.

The ride went on and on, the car weaving in and out of the slower moving traffic. Iris, having no idea how far they were going, kept her hands on the wheel. It felt better, more like real life and less like a science-fiction movie, to at least pretend there was someone in control of the car. The van got off one freeway and onto another, then off that one and onto back roads. The driver-less car was right behind. They passed through the familiar towns of Iris's home region. Snohomish, Woodinville, Duval. They skirted the major population centers of Marysville, Everett and Bothell and ended up in Juanita.

Quite a roundabout route, Iris thought, trying to keep her jerking and gasping to a minimum. To the other drivers around her she must look like she had Tourette's. And through it all

Trammel did not speak again. Iris hoped the vile woman wasn't cooking up some nefarious plan to get rid of Iris and her friends.

She had to find a way to get them all out of this predicament. With the long silence, and beginning to get control of herself, she fell into a daydream of ways she could get in control and away from Gloria Trammel. Once she'd done that, she could go get her friends out of their prison. Mona had not looked good. She wanted to get her to a doctor as soon as possible.

Her sister had taken such a sudden turn for the worse. Was it just the stress of this outlandish predicament Iris had landed them in? She felt like a complete fool for mixing things up. She'd never meant to steal Trammel's bag. She had to find a way to correct her terrible error.

But Trammel had the bag now, she had her money back, and still she was holding Iris at gun point and her friends as prisoners. Why hadn't she let them go? They were no threat to her.

Whatever Trammel's motives for holding them, Iris had to take action. But to do anything at all she would first have to get control of this car. Maybe she could cause a crash. That would stop things and get the police here. But she couldn't make the car do what she wanted. She took a deep breath. The first step was to control herself and stop hyperventilating about this crazy car and this terrible woman and turn her attention to analyzing what was going on. She began to think calming thoughts.

Trammel seemed to be controlling the vehicle with her voice. The woman had not touched any of the controls that Iris could see. It had only done things Trammel had said out loud, and that hadn't been much. It didn't respond at all to Iris' continued yips of fright when it changed lanes or sped up. She just couldn't help saying, "Slow down." She'd always been a backseat driver. Ken, bless him, had stoically put up with it all their married life. Amy, on the other hand, hated it and was pretty vocal about how much.

Their tour of Europe had been filled with bickering over Iris' bad habit.

Though it didn't talk back, the car was like that contraption Amy kept on her kitchen counter. She told it to set timers for baking, and to play music. Iris was perfectly happy setting her Mickey Mouse timer with her actual hand, thank you very much. But now, if she was going to do anything to get herself out of this terrible situation, it was time to let go of her phobias and figure out this technology.

Of course, Iris could not try to take control by giving the car voice commands out loud. Trammel would hear her and simply contradict any directions she gave the machine. She decided to continue yipping, stomping the imaginary brake, and otherwise expressing fear while she read all the sections of the monitor, and watched what was happening to each.

There was a map that was keeping track of where they were. Superimposed on that was a diagram that showed the cars around them, including the van that Trammel had told the autonomous vehicle to follow. There were digital representations of a speedometer, odometer, etcetera, and something that looked like it might be a power gauge.

Iris was good at puzzles, and slowly she put together all the icons and readouts. The key element took her a while to figure out. There was no button labeled manual control. Instead, there was a small gray button on top of the steering wheel, where it would not be inadvertently touched by either the driver or the passenger.

When Trammel was busy texting, Iris tapped the button. A line of text appeared at the top of the screen. Voice Control OFF.

Just looking at those few words made Iris' throat constrict and her heart beat faster again. She took a deep breath to calm herself, cleared her throat and said, "Look at that lake."

Trammel dutifully turned and looked at the lake. But only for an instant. Iris tapped the button again. Voice Control ON.

"It's so beautiful." She would rattle on about the surroundings and her life, as a woman like Trammel would expect of an old woman. Be boring, and be frightened. Keep Trammel firmly in her ageist comfort zone. No doubt the lake was boring for her, an everyday thing. Iris could tell she was bored by the way she glanced at it and then back down to her phone. How horrible to be so jaded by the expectation of beauty and luxury. What a way to live.

"I went to school in Seattle, but my husband and I had a house out here. In Kirkland, actually. Near the lake. The kids were always out in boats like that."

Gingerly, seeming reluctant, she took a hand off the wheel and pointed at a boat skimming across the sparkling water. She described the boats they'd had.

"Then when the kids were little we got a small fishing boat like that one. I was never all that much for boating, but Ken loved it. We'd putt around on weekends and let the kids catch a trout or two. Sometimes we'd tow them on an inner tube. Then when they were older we bought them a ski boat. They'd take their friends out water skiing every day all summer. Ken and I – that was my husband's name, Ken – we'd go from here over to Lake Forest Park or Bothell for dinner sometimes." She smiled to punctuate the nice feeling she was trying to build. "Those were good days."

There was no response.

"I remember the sunsets from here were gorgeous, too. Those clouds low on the horizon might make for a nice sunset tonight."

Perhaps Trammel liked sunsets, because she finally turned her head enough for Iris to reach out and tap the button again. And then the other button she'd identified. The autopilot button. As she touched it, her throat seized up. Her hair felt like it was standing on end in fear of the crazy thing she was doing. The car

116

slowed slightly, pedals descended as if by magic. Holding her breath, Iris carefully lifted her foot and applied it to the one that appeared where the gas should be and was pleasantly surprised to be able to smoothly bring the car back up to speed. Trammel seemed not to have noticed, just went back to her texting. Iris let her breath out slowly, silently.

Iris needed to keep her captor looking around, though, because an icon had appeared that showed a person steering.

"Our favorite bait shop used to be right there where that green and black condo is now." She chuckled, then yelped as she sped up a little. "It still freaks me out when it does that." She blew out a breath.

Heart hammering, she changed lanes on a wide corner. It looked like she was still behind the van, but she was actually now in the lane that would take the next exit. The van's brake lights came on as the driver tapped them to slow. No doubt Sunshine and Helen were wondering what was going on. What would the sisters do now? She hoped they didn't call Trammel right away to ask why she was no longer following. Had their allegiance really switched back to their vile boss, or could she count on them to help her and her friends?

She laughed softly and went on talking, trying to keep Trammel distracted.

"I remember that bait shop was so smelly. Unlike that big elegant edifice, it was a little orange hovel. Made of cement block, if I recall correctly. I hated the bait part. And cleaning the fish. That was smelly and messy. I bet a lady like you has never been out fishing in a little boat. You do have to really like fish to put up with the smell and to enjoy sitting all day with a line in the water waiting for them to bite." She laughed a little nervously and steered the car onto the surface street, raced through a yellow light, took a left, and quickly put them back on the freeway going back the way they'd come.

While facing resolutely forward, Iris glanced out of the side of her eye and watched Trammel physically shake off the hypnotic trance the reminiscences seemed to have put her in. Iris smiled. Perhaps the woman had a memory of a lovely time on the water as a child. But then she came alive, looking around her in a puzzled way. Then she turned back to Iris and raised the gun again.

"What the hell do you think you're doing?"

"Just passing the time," Iris voice squeaked a little as it squeezed past her clenched vocal chords. "Telling stories is a good way to get to know one another. Where did you grow up, dear? Here in the Seattle area?"

"Stop," Trammel commanded, and put her hand on the dash. "Pull over to the shoulder." She waited a beat, then narrowed her eyes at Iris.

"You figured out how to take control of the vehicle."

"Oh?" said Iris, "Am I driving?"

"Very funny."

Iris still didn't look directly at the woman, but another side wise glance told her Trammel's eyes had turned mean. The socialite's voice dropped to a hiss. "I thought you didn't know anything about self-driving cars."

"I don't," said Iris. "Well, I know a little more now." She smiled and risked turning toward Trammel. "Did you forget a basic fact of life? Old people enjoy crosswords, Sudoku and jigsaws." She shrugged. "I figured it out."

"I see. I have an octogenarian genius at the wheel of my car." Trammel leaned back, nonchalant again. "So tell me, genius, how is your knowledge of guns?" She smiled in her superior, unkind way.

"I'm not eighty." Iris was incensed. "I'm a septuagenarian. And while I might not be a firearms expert, I know that if a gun goes off while I'm driving sixty miles per hour, bad things will happen to my passenger. It's in every heist movie. And that's what this is, right? Some kind of slow motion heist?"

"How charming," Trammel said. "I've taken hostage a fan of the big ticket robbery genre." She grinned again, positively glowing with pride. "Hollywood has done me a great favor hyping those casino take down stories. That's the kind of thing security focuses on, which leaves me free to run my operations."

My god, thought Iris, the woman is preening.

"Really?" she said breathily, hoping to sound thrilled and worshipful. "How do you do your robberies?"

"I do not rob anyone." The woman's voice hardened.

Crap. "Sorry. I'm not actually sure what you do. The girl at the front desk mentioned fashion videos. When they were showing you that beautiful cake this morning. Are you a model?"

"In a sense, yes. I am a role model." Trammel tipped her head, smiled as if for a camera, and sat up straighter.

"I'm sorry, I still don't get it. From what I understand, you take pictures of yourself putting on makeup. It's not like you're curing cancer."

"I might as well be. The cancer of self-doubt. I provide women with confidence. Young women need an example of how to use their influence with subtlety and polish. They look to me for guidance in how to keep from becoming . . . ordinary." Her mouth twitched and she actually tipped her head back and looked down her nose at Iris. Whose blood returned to the boiling point.

"As I mentioned," she went on. "I work leverage."

"Oh, I see," said Iris, who actually still had little clue what that meant. She went back to driving, and thinking about what to do next. Slowing, she eased the car into the thickening, northbound rush hour traffic. Tone down the venom, Iris, she told herself.

She smiled sweetly, rolled down the windows and smiled at the driver in the car to her right. Trammel jumped and lowered the gun. "I know how to use leverage, too. All I have to do is keep on driving. Stay right here in the flow of traffic so that you have a large audience, should you try anything stupid. This time of day, I think we'll be in heavy traffic all the way to the Canadian border." She tilted her head as the thought occurred to her. "Come to think of it, that would be an excellent place to stop."

CHAPTER 12

"Helen, the car is gone."

"What?" Helen checked back and forth between her mirrors, scanning the road behind her. "What is Gloria up to now?"

"Maybe that white SUV pulled in between us," said Sunshine. "She's probably behind that. She'll come roaring around it any second."

"Roaring," said Helen. They both laughed.

But Gloria's car didn't appear.

"Change lanes, see if you can get a glimpse behind these other cars."

Helen did, and they both searched the traffic behind them, then ahead of them for the gold electric prototype.

"Where could she have gone? As suspicious as she was back there at the house, she should be right on our tail like a metal-flake nightmare."

"Are you still getting texts?"

"Nothing for several minutes."

"Should we call her to see what's going on?"

"Call Gloria?" Sunshine shook her head emphatically. "No. No way. Gloria silent is exactly the way I like her."

A mile later, when the gold car had still not reappeared and they'd had no word from Gloria Trammel, Sunshine and Helen took stock.

"We're only a mile or so from the storage unit. Let's just go there as planned. She must have taken a shortcut," said Sunshine.

"And if she's not there?"

"Then I vote we go back to the house, see if she's there."

"Why on earth would she go back there? You think she's had a change of heart? Decided to be nice to the old ladies?"

"Without telling us. Yeah, probably not. She'd have some other, more self-serving reason. But if she's not there we can let Amanda, Emily, and Mona out and call them an Uber."

"Great idea. At least get them out of Gloria's clutches. Though I think Mona needs an ambulance rather than an Uber."

"True."

Helen took the exit toward Trammel's storage unit. "I wonder what she's done with the other one. I forget her name."

"The hostage? Iris," said Sunshine, staring out the side window. "Yeah, nothing good, I'm afraid."

***

Amanda and Emily had finished grieving for now. Mona had died about an hour ago, without regaining consciousness. She'd moaned, and whispered in her sleep, but they hadn't been able to pick out more than a few words. Carry. Iris. Mother. Strong. She seemed to be focused on strong women carrying things.

After they wiped away the tears, they each said a few words, then they covered her face with the lovely scarf she'd been so proud of. Next they'd gone through a scared stage, wondering if they, too, were going to die in this barren bedroom.

Now they were just pissed off. And they both needed to use the facilities.

The four friends had thought they'd brought the young sisters, Sunshine and Helen, over to their side. But then Gloria Trammel had waltzed in, and with hardly a word of discussion, the young women had gone off to do her bidding, abandoning a dying woman.

Emily was ready to kill anyone who walked through the door. Amanda was more on the maim side herself, but she definitely looked forward to inflicting plenty of pain.

They'd rearranged the room to suit their purposes, wondering several times what the sisters used such a spartan bedroom for. There was nothing in it but the bed, the rug, and the chair the two had originally used to bring Mona from the van. Now they were working at the lock with a comb they'd found when they rolled up the rug to use as a trip hazard. It was the only tool they'd come across in their search for a way out.

"It's no use," said Amanda, heaving herself to her feet and shaking her numb legs. "The teeth are too flexible, they just bend when I try to pry with them."

"Alright," Emily held out her hand. "Time to try pulling the pins."

"With the door closed? We discussed this. I really don't think . . ."

"Shut it Amanda, I'm going to try. We're not going to do ourselves, or Iris, any good just sitting here. And personally I want to keep my mind busy and off . . .," her eyes drifted to the form on the bed.

Amanda closed her eyes and nodded.

"Get the chair."

Amanda crossed the room and grasped the chair back, then stopped and, with effort, climbed up on it again. "Maybe it's time to break the window and shout for help," she said, looking around the fenced backyard, and over the fence to the river. "I can see the roof of a house on either side. They don't seem too far away."

"For god's sake, be careful, Amanda. I don't need another dead body on my hands."

"That's no way to speak about Mona," said Amanda, as she eased herself back down to the floor. "You're making me cross with your callous attitude. She was our friend."

"Shhh," Emily jumped to her feet. "Someone's coming."

Amanda stopped breathing. But she picked up the chair and tiptoed across to the door. She took up her position at the knob side, ready to swing with everything she had. Emily stood toward the hinge side, poised to fling her body against the opening door and knock their captors off their feet. It was two to two this time, not great odds for her and Emily. But they would do what they could.

"Emily! Amanda! Mona?" Someone was shouting and running through the house.

"Are you alright?" came another voice. "The ambulance is on its way."

"It's Helen and Sunshine," said Amanda, lowering the chair.

Emily frowned. "Stay tough, Amanda. We can't trust them. It might be a trick."

"That doesn't make any sense. Why would they need to trick us when they have the keys and all the power?"

The door began to rattle as a key was inserted.

"I don't know. But I'm going to assume the worst until I can disprove my theory."

Amanda rolled her eyes. But as the door opened, she swung the chair and connected with something.

"Ooof," said Helen, dropping backward onto her butt and clutching her mid-section.

"Amanda, why did you do . . ." said Sunshine just before Emily smashed the door into her shoulder.

Amanda and Emily didn't wait around for any more discussion. They stepped over the fallen women and hustled down the hall. A wailing sound came from the front of the house.

"The police?" said Amanda. "We're saved!"

"Amanda, we are not saved," Emily barked. "We're mixed up in a casino theft. The police are not our friends right now. What we are, is trapped."

A moment later the four of them faced off around the kitchen table. Amanda brandished another chair. Emily had a butcher knife. There was pounding on the door.

As they circled the table, Sunshine was trying to convince them everything was okay. "We're on your side, really. We lost Gloria and we called an ambulance."

"That's the paramedics for Mona," said Helen, pointing to the front door, "not the police."

"We're not quite ready for the police," said Sunshine. "We're worried about Iris."

"We are, too," Amanda said, wheezing so badly she had to lean on the chair she'd been intending to use as a weapon. "If you lost Gloria, you also lost our friend."

"She needs her inhaler," Emily said, glaring and brandishing the knife at each of the sisters in turn. "Which you took when you jumped us after the accident."

The pounding started again. Then the bell rang.

Helen held up her hands. "Let's all be calm." She went to a closet and took out a bunch of purses. "Would it be in one of these?"

Amanda reached for the yellow bag, found the medicine, and took a hit.

Helen nodded and headed to the door, returning a moment later leading two uniformed men with medical kits. "The ambulance is here for Mona." The men looked around the room. They seemed to scrutinize every detail and Amanda struggled to breathe normally. She brushed imaginary crumbs off the seat of the chair and slid it into place under the table. Emily turned and pretended to dry the knife on the kitchen towel.

"It's too late, I'm afraid," Amanda said quietly to Sunshine. "But thank you for trying."

"Thanks for nothing," shouted Emily, sliding the knife back into the block. "You let her die when you could have done something."

"Emily, please, you're distraught," said Amanda, trying to keep her breathing under control. "You know no one could have done anything. She was very ill."

When the paramedics were out of earshot Sunshine dropped her voice to a whisper. "I'm so very sorry. We didn't think anyone would get hurt. But if we'd called for the ambulance while Gloria was here, she'd have shot Iris. That wouldn't have done anything to help Mona."

"It's not your fault," said Amanda. "Mona didn't get hurt. She was sick well before she arrived in town to visit Iris."

"The paramedics need a bunch of information," Helen said as she came back into the room. "What was it Mona had, do you know?"

"A brain tumor."

Emily gaped at Amanda. "How did you know that?"

"She told me when we were out walking. She came to spend her last days with Iris. To say goodbye. She also hoped that Iris could help her find her estranged daughter before the end."

"That's so sad," said Sunshine. There was a catch in her voice.

Helen nodded. "Okay. And they want to know how long it has been since . . . well, since you thought she died?"

"Cripes, I don't know," said Emily, palm to face. "I've had a lot on my mind. Maybe it's been about an hour."

"At least that. I'd say closer to two," said Amanda.

"We haven't been gone that long," said Helen. "But they're going to wonder why we waited so long to call for help."

They sat in sad silence for a moment, then Helen sighed. "We can't tell the whole truth. If they ask, I'll figure out some excuse." She went to report all this to the paramedics.

"Cripes," said Emily again. "They're going to want to know if she has a Do Not Resuscitate order. Otherwise they have to try to save her life."

Amanda felt faint. "Oh, no. I never thought of that. What are we going to do?"

One of the paramedics came into the kitchen. The four women cringed slightly. "I'm afraid it's too late for us to do anything for your friend."

Emily sighed and nodded. "We knew that."

"We were with her when she died," said Amanda. Emily frowned at her and she shut her mouth.

He wanted all Mona's personal information. They gave him what they could, which was her first name. Then they had to admit they knew basically nothing else about her. They didn't even know Mona's last name.

"We only met her this morning," said Emily.

They didn't know where she lived.

"She came from out of town somewhere, to visit her sister," said Amanda.

The medic wrote that down, while the other three women turned wide eyes on her. Amanda knew immediately what they were thinking. She should not have mentioned a sister. Now they would want to know about Iris.

"You need her ID?" Emily stammered as she tried to answer. "Well . . . um . . . she doesn't have it . . . um . . . with her? Maybe in her purse?"

"Where is her purse?" Emily was repeating everything the medic said. She turned to the others. "Where is Mona's purse? Does anyone know if she had a purse?"

Amanda opened her mouth to answer, but Emily kept right on going, shaking her head, talking, glaring at Amanda. Amanda shut her mouth and shook her head. The money. Of course they had to say they didn't know.

Emily turned back to the medic. "No. I don't think I ever saw her purse, so we can't help you there." Amanda was amazed at how smoothly she lied. But then, she had spent years as a vice president of a major corporation.

"Would it be one of those?" They all looked where he was pointing

"N-no," stammered Emily, staring at the heap on the chair. "Those are all ours."

The medic sighed. "Well, we'll just have to contact her sister then. Does one of you have her name and number?"

Emily was just about to answer when the other medic came into the room pulling off his gloves. "She's ready for transport."

The women all breathed a sigh of relief at the interruption. Good lord, thought Amanda, they sounded like they were glad to get rid of Mona. She hoped the officers assumed it was grief. "It's so sad," she said, in an effort to cover. "Thank you for trying to help."

"My condolences ladies. I'm very sorry about your friend. If you could give us the sister's information someone will contact her for funeral arrangements."

"Oh, my god," said Amanda again. "Poor Iris."

Emily got up, crossed to the chair that was laden with bags, opened her backpack and took out her phone. She slowly scrolled to the end for Iris' number. "Her name is Iris Winterbek. Her number is 555-555-5555."

The medic wrote down the information and the two men went back into the bedroom.

"Did you hear that?" said Amanda. "They're going to transport. So we won't have to take her in Iris' car. That's a huge relief."

"Why is that?" said Helen, blinking.

"Iris was adamant this morning. No dead bodies allowed in her car."

Sunshine and Helen both leaned back in their chairs as if trying to put space between themselves and Amanda. They exchanged a glance. Hesitantly, Sunshine spoke. "Why were you discussing transporting dead bodies in Iris' car?"

"Were you planning on someone dying today?" said Helen.

"Birds," croaked Emily. "We were only talking about birds. For heaven's sake, Amanda, one time, could you think before you speak?" Emily dropped her chin onto her open palm and gaped across the table. "Now you have them thinking we're a bunch of serial killers."

CHAPTER 13

"What are we going to do now?" asked Amanda.

The four women sat looking at one another, then Sunshine hopped to her feet and crossed to the stove. "I think we could all use a cup of tea."

A phone started to ring and they all jumped and turned to look at the chair in the corner and the lavender tote that peeked out from under the pile of other baggage.

"Oh, hell," said Emily. "I forgot about that."

"Quick," said Amanda, pushing everything off and holding the lavender bag out to Sunshine. "You're faster, take it outside before they hear. Turn it off or let it go to voice-mail. That will buy us time."

Helen headed to the bedroom to keep the paramedics occupied.

"They left a message for the sister," she said when she returned. "The coroner will be here within the hour."

"I shut off the phone," said Sunshine, shoving the lavender bag back under the pile.

"Do we have to stay here and wait?" said Emily.

"As the homeowners, one of us probably has to, but you can go."

"How can we go?" demanded Amanda.

"I'm calling an Uber right now," said Emily. "Then the towing company, to meet us out there. We need to see if they can get Iris' car out of the woods."

"Can you do that if you're not the owner?" said Amanda.

"I don't know. But we've got Iris' driver's license. I'll pretend to be her. Young men think all old women look alike. We're about the same size, anyway. I'll just tell them I stopped dying my hair that sickly yellow."

Helen came back into the kitchen. "They don't seem to think it's a suspicious death," she said. "No talk about calling anyone but the coroner, who has to sign off on the death certificate."

"Imagine doing that all day," said Emily. "Yuck."

"Oh my god," wailed Amanda. "This can't go on. Sooner or later someone is going to end up calling the police."

Helen's eyes slid back and forth between them. "Should we keep it quiet?"

Amanda nodded. "It's not a suspicious death." Then she frowned and slowly turned to Emily. "On second thought. Maybe we should be the ones to call the police. We need to report what Gloria Trammel forced Helen and Sunshine to do. And Mona only died here in their house because of her."

"But then we have to wait for the police," said Emily. "I've been here long enough, thank you very much."

"But Emily, that's a good thing," said Amanda. "We need the police."

"Why do we need them?"

"Have you forgotten that Iris has been kidnapped by Gloria Trammel, who evaded Sunshine and Helen, and is now missing?"

"She's right." Sunshine nodded, but she looked terrified. "We have to tell the police." The young sisters exchanged a look and in unison let out a matching pair of sighs.

"Wait," Amanda was having second thoughts. "If you do that, you and Helen will be implicated in Trammel's scheme. You'll go to jail. Then it will all get very complicated."

Emily put her hands on her hips. "I don't care about any of that. I want to know where that terrible woman has taken Iris. You were awfully willing to go back to work for her. We watched you all go off together. How do we know you're telling us the truth about her just disappearing?"

"Emily, please believe us," Sunshine made praying hands. "I know it must be hard to trust us after all this, but really, we don't know where she's gone. Other than casinos, we only ever met her in three places – Gloria's storage unit, our house, and her office, which is in a Bellevue high-rise. Not exactly a place to take a hostage. I've never even been to her house. We don't know where she lives. I've tried to find a listing, but there's nothing for her or her husband anywhere. And we're telling the truth. They were following us to the storage unit when the car just disappeared."

Helen nodded. "We were on the freeway. They were behind us. When Sun said the car was gone, I thought maybe they'd got cut off, so I slowed down and switched lanes to see if they were behind another car or two. But they'd just vanished."

"Where was this?"

"Down near Kirkland."

"What? That's a million miles away," Amanda was wailing now. "We can't search all that area."

"Did you call to see what happened?"

"Are you kidding?" Helen was emphatic. "We were free of Gloria Trammel. We weren't going to get her on our tail again."

Sunshine pulled out her phone. "She did finally send us a text. Look at this note. It's too cryptic for me."

She held up her phone for the others to read.

"On I-5 to hangover. Fin us new."

"I don't understand," said Amanda.

"It's gotta be a typo and spellcheck fixed it wrong," said Helen.

"Effing spellcheck," said Emily.

"Hangover . . . Hannover? What around here starts with H?" said Amanda.

"Not much. Hartstene Island," said Emily.

"The Highlands," said Helen.

"Hood Canal," said Sunshine.

"Humptulips," said Amanda.

"Hold on. Work with the rest of the word. H . . .ve," said Emily.

"Hover? Hoverton, Hoverville," said Helen.

"Hoover?" Sunshine sounded excited for a second and then subsided. "No, there's no Hoover in Washington. Hoover Dam is in Nevada."

Emily's eyes got wide. "Hanford? Does she have any connection to the nuclear plant?"

"God, I hope not." Sunshine gave a nervous laugh. "I hate to think of Gloria Trammel with her finger on that button."

They sat in silence for a moment. Then one of the paramedics came out and told them the coroner was a minute away and they were about ready to transport. They all jumped up and stood wringing their hands. There was another knock at the door. The paramedics went to answer it.

"Vancouver," hissed Amanda.

The other three women turned puzzled faces her way.

"The text message. The word that ends in ver. Gloria and Iris are on the way to Vancouver."

"Good job, Amanda. But that's not really a big help," said Emily. "Vancouver, Washington or Vancouver, British Columbia? They're in two different directions."

"Do we go north or south?" said Helen, palms up.

"Ahhh," said Amanda, putting her hands on the sides of her head. "Why would they be going to either Vancouver if you expected them to go to Kirkland, which is half way in between?"

"I don't know, but clearly we'll have to split up," said Sunshine.

"It can't be B. C. They'd never get across the border. Iris doesn't have ID," said Emily.

"Oh my god! Iris will get taken into custody by border security!" Amanda couldn't stop herself falling into wail mode again. Her emotions were raw.

"Cripes, Amanda, will you shut up?"

"Hold on a moment," said Amanda, a sudden thought helping her recover. "What did that text say again?"

Helen quoted. "On I-5 to hangover. Fin us new."

Amanda nodded. "That's what I thought. And now I'm wondering, why would Gloria Trammel need you to find her on I-5, regardless of which direction she was going?"

They all stared at one another.

When she spoke, Helen's voice was full of awe. "Amanda, you nailed it. Gloria doesn't have control of the car."

Sunshine threw up her hands. "That's ridiculous, Helen. It's self-driving. I think she somehow programs in where she wants it to go."

"She told me she can also set it for voice command."

"Of course, the human driver can take over and control it manually, too, so . . ."

Emily interrupted, looking intently at the ceiling. "Who was in the driver's seat when they left the house?"

"Ohhhhh . . . "said Amanda, Sunshine and Helen in unison.

"Iris has control of the car," said Sunshine through gritted teeth, as a dignified, gray-haired woman entered, followed by the paramedics.

The four friends put a cap on their glee, answered some more questions, then stood respectfully as the trio wheeled Mona past.

"How long until the battery runs out?" asked Emily as the officials disappeared around the corner.

"What happens when the battery runs out?" asked Amanda, as they all followed to see Mona out the front door.

"We can't wait for all that," Emily whispered. "And we don't need the police. All we have to do is go get Iris' car out of the ditch. Then we have to find Iris. My money is on Vancouver, B.C.. Iris would head there because they'd be stopped at the border, which would give her a chance to escape. But Trammel will have other ideas. Sunshine, you have to call that monster and find out where they are."

Sunshine nodded sadly as the four of them waved to the coroner and the paramedics and the two white vans drove away. "But first, we have to go get your car."

They went back inside to collect all the bags and check to make sure they hadn't left anything in the bedroom. Then they went to the garage.

Amanda stood looking into the van filled with boxes. "Those are all full of money?"

"Some are," said Helen.

"There are no seats," said Amanda.

"Sorry," said Helen. "We'd let you sit up front, but if Gloria happened to be headed this way and saw you, our plan would break down."

"My car is at the casino," said Sunshine. "This is all we've got."

"You want us to sit on boxes?" asked Emily. "With nothing to hold on to? That doesn't sound very safe to me."

Sunshine turned and rummaged in a pile of boxes and came up with two bed pillows. "Here, it's not much, but you can sit on these."

She helped Emily and Amanda get in the van again, a much gentler process this time.

"You'd better take it easy on the corners," said Emily sounding none too happy.

CHAPTER 14

Traffic was getting worse as Iris steered north on Highway 405 to join up with Interstate 5. It would come nearly to a halt once they were on the main line, but she was determined to keep going and stay in control until she could think of something else. She was getting madder at Gloria Trammel by the minute. Her day of fun and gambling was fast disappearing, her friends were in trouble, and Mona . . . Mona was in deep trouble. She seemed almost lifeless at times, then she rallied. Iris had to find some way to get her to the hospital. She had to come up with a plan.

Think, old woman, think!

"I know what you're thinking. You think you can take control of this situation," said Trammel finally, jolting Iris with the word she'd just been repeating to herself.

The blond woman was leaning back against the passenger side door studying Iris, the gun nonchalantly lying in her lap, though her finger was still on the trigger and the business end was still pointed at Iris' midsection. The situation, from Iris' point of view, was a repeat of that frightening afternoon in Ireland, when the smuggler, Hal Smith had kidnapped her. Except Hal, being a large, strong man, had driven himself, with one bulky arm clamped around Iris' arms. Also, Hal's actions had at least had a point. He'd wanted something from her. So far, Gloria Trammel didn't seem to have any reason at all for holding her.

"What exactly is this situation, in your mind?" Iris asked sweetly. "I have to admit, dear, you have me quite puzzled. Why am I here, instead of locked up with my friends? What did you gain by taking me hostage? Surely you weren't looking for a getaway driver."

Gloria Trammel grinned. If one could call the overstretched rictus of an aging debutante a grin. Grimace? Leer? Really there ought to be more words for the many kinds of smiles there were in this world, and the many things they could mean. Grin would have to do, as Iris didn't have time to worry about finding a better word.

"Oh," drawled Trammel. "That was a joke. I get it." She play slapped Iris's arm. "That was witty. Because you knew I already had a better driver than you could ever hope to be." She laughed. "But this is too funny. You fancy you've fallen into the plot of some elaborate robbery, don't you? You must be absolutely thrilled. You need to take a reality break, lady. If I did want someone to drive my getaway car, I certainly wouldn't choose a mousy old crone who can't turn her head."

"I can turn my head," said Iris, demonstrating for the bitch.

"Oh, snap." Trammel laughed again. "Look at that. Such skill. Such agility. I bet you can even see out the driver's side mirror. Turning right gives you more trouble though. Luckily you don't have to back this car."

Iris was getting irritated with this bitch. Why did some people feel the need to put others down at every opportunity? She simply did not see the point in that kind of thinking.

"Do you get your jollies by hurting people any way you can?"

"My jollies?" Trammel laughed again, her red mouth wide. "You are such a throwback! But sure, I enjoy discomfiting people who can't be of use in other ways." Trammel looked toward the road ahead, with something almost like wistfulness. "Yes. Yes, I do."

Iris tried again. "If I'm of no use, then I repeat, why did you kidnap me? I refuse to believe you kidnapped me just to have someone to verbally abuse."

"You were right the first time. I didn't kidnap you, I took you hostage. There's a difference."

Iris was getting exasperated with the stupid woman and her games. Why was she so calm, when Iris had taken control of the car and upended all her plans? She gave an exasperated sigh. "Well, excuse me. Why did you take me hostage?"

"Your sister, of course. The others had only each other. You had them and your dear sister. You offered the most leverage." Trammel looked at her again and shrugged. "I prefer maximum leverage."

It was more the way the woman said the word than the word itself that made Iris' mouth go dry. Trammel just seemed to want to toy with her, and was not at all inconvenienced by loss of control. Which meant she was still in control, somehow. Did she have something else up her sleeve? Maybe she had another way to take control of the car and was just letting Iris dig a hole for herself. Iris ran her eyes over the dash in front of Trammel. There was nothing. No button, no control that she could see.

This was just too much stress. Iris couldn't take much more. Maybe that was all Trammel was banking on, Iris' old nerves giving out before she could get to safety. She wished she had a Tic Tac. Her mouth felt like, if she tried to spit, all that would come out would be sawdust. She felt around in the pockets of her slacks. Then her jacket pockets. No Tic Tac. All she had was Emily's little bottle of hand sanitizer, which she'd picked up from the floor of the van. Emily must have dropped it when the sisters stuffed them all inside. Yuck. It was probably coated with bird guts. Iris wiped her hand on her pants. She'd meant to give it back, but with one thing and another, she'd forgotten again.

CHAPTER 15

Standing at the side of the road, Emily and Amanda watched the tow truck's powerful winch inch Iris's car out of the woods. The young sisters stood nearby, whispering nervously.

"Iris is very lucky she didn't hit a tree," said Amanda. "There are so many of them, but she managed to go right between them all."

"Stick with the luck theory," said Emily. "Iris didn't manage anything."

"You don't think she chose this place as the best if she had to run off the road?"

"I don't think she chose, no. And she didn't have to run off the road. Her inability to decide which way to turn was the whole problem."

"Oh, right," said Amanda. "I'd forgotten that part."

"What?" asked Sunshine, looking over at them. "Iris didn't lose control of the vehicle?"

"Um," said Amanda. "She just seemed to go kind of slow right here at the T, not sure which way to go. But I don't think she took her foot off the gas."

"She lost control all right, but of her decision-making apparatus, not the car."

Helen started to giggle. "And she just drove off the road while she was trying to decide? I assumed she was going too fast, trying to lose us."

"That's wild!" said Sunshine, laughing now, too.

"That's Iris," said Emily. "Sometimes she's a few sandwiches short of a picnic."

"And other times she runs rings around you, Em." Amanda turned to Helen. "Don't ever bet against Iris in a game of Sudoku."

"I hope she's okay," said Sunshine. "I can't figure out why Gloria took her."

"I think she just wanted to be mean," said Helen. "She found the most vulnerable person in the room and twisted the knife, so to speak."

Sunshine shrugged. "That's my guess too. She's like that."

"That's exactly what you don't want to do to Iris," said Emily. "She's at her very best, her most effective when she's angry at injustice."

"Well, I'm not sure it's really that she's at her best. What happens is she throws caution to the winds, and everybody has to watch out," said Amanda. "While I'm worried about her, I'm actually really curious what kind of mayhem she will bring down on Gloria Trammel. Especially when she learns Mona has died."

They all took a collective sigh of sadness. But before they could fall into recriminations or what ifs, the whining winch stopped. They all turned their attention back to the car, which was out of the underbrush, and to the open verge of the road. The driver was adjusting the hook to bring it up the slight embankment.

"How is it?" Helen asked the man. "Any damage?"

"I didn't see anything but a few scratches from broken branches. The front wheels are rolling fine," he said. "So that's a good sign."

The car now on the tarmac, the driver unhooked the winch and attached tow cables. He hopped in his truck, and after some fancy maneuvering he had the little green Honda faced the right way and came to join the four women as they walked around it, inspecting.

"I'll start it up, shall I?" said Emily and got in. The engine leapt to life. She gave a thumbs-up and stuck her head out the window. "I'm going to drive forward a bit, then back up to see if everything works."

Everything did work. Emily turned the car around a couple of times, just to be sure, then paid the driver. As he drove away, she turned to the sisters.

"I guess this is goodbye. Thank you for – well almost everything – everything from the time you arrived back at the house without Gloria, at least." She stuck out her hand.

"What are you talking about?" said Amanda. "This is not goodbye."

All eyes turned to her and she felt her face get hot. Now she was going to have to say something intelligent. "Um. What I mean is, we can't just go our own ways. First of all, what is our way from here Emily? Just go home? Don't forget we still need to locate Iris and get her away from that fashionable fiend. I think we'll need help with that."

"Well, we discussed this. They are going to call Gloria and locate her, and I was going to call the police," said Emily.

Amanda shook her head. "The police will just say they don't do missing persons cases until they've been missing for twenty-four hours or something. I'm waiting right here while Sunshine calls Gloria to see where they are. Once we know that we can make a plan to get Iris back, or call the police."

Helen and Sunshine looked at each other. Helen nodded. Then they both turned serious gazes back to Emily and Amanda.

"We made one more decision while you were working with the tow truck driver," said Sunshine. "Actually, we talk all the time about how to get out of this terrible situation with Gloria. But today things escalated with all of you and then Gloria barging in. We worked on it when we were heading to the storage unit, and after we lost her. We've finally decided what to do."

"Yep," said Helen, taking over and shaking her fist in the air. "It's just time to say damn the torpedoes. We have to end Gloria's reign of terror over these poor casino workers she's targeted for blackmail. We're going to turn ourselves and the money in and tell the whole story."

"It'll be quite sensational." Sunshine looked a little nervous and grimaced. "The internet loves it when one of their online darlings is revealed to be a hypocrite."

"It's going to be mighty uncomfortable for us too, Babe," said Helen, putting her arm around Sunshine's shoulders.

"But what about Grandmother Femke?" said Amanda. "You have to get the money to protect that precious work of art."

"Oh, for cripes' sake," said Emily, rolling her eyes. "Are you seriously suggesting these girls continue their life of crime working for a blackmailer? Get some perspective. It's paint on fabric, and the woman has been dead for three hundred years. What they need to protect is living people who are in danger from Gloria Trammel right now."

"And what if those people are just as bad as she is?" Amanda had had just about enough of Emily's sniping at her love of art. She put her hands on her hips and drew herself up to full height, towering a full inch over Emily. "She wouldn't be able to blackmail them if she didn't have evidence they were doing something underhanded."

Sunshine broke in, making a T out of her hands in between them. "Time out, ladies. Regardless of whether anyone else has done anything wrong, we need to take this money back to the casino and clear our own names."

"They'll go easier on us if we turn Gloria in and return the money," said Helen.

"Don't be too sure of that," said Emily. "I have experience with – um – influential people. They don't let go of anything easily. She'll fight you."

"She's probably got everything rigged so if you rat on her she shows them evidence that it was all your idea."

"Oh, Jesus," said Emily, frowning at Amanda. "Someone has been watching too much CSI."

Helen cleared her throat loudly, and the two friends looked at her.

"There are a couple of other things that tipped our decision in favor of coming clean."

"Oh?" said Amanda, surprised at the apologetic tone of Helen's voice and the sheepish look on Sunshine's face.

"Like what?" Emily demanded, folding her arms.

"It just doesn't seem right, Helen," said Sunshine, holding her sister's eyes.

"I know, Sun. It seems so mercenary."

"Plus, there's no one here to corroborate our story."

"Cripes," said Emily. "CSI again? Out with it."

Sunshine shook her head and blew out her held breath. "Just go ahead, Helen. They have to know."

"Iris told us . . ." she stopped and gestured toward the van. "This could take a while. Why don't we sit down." Helen opened the sliding door and sat. The others wandered over. Emily and Amanda sat, but Sunshine said she was fine standing. She looked very fidgety and nervous.

Helen cleared her throat. "It was just before Gloria burst in. Mona was sleeping. We were talking about a plan for raiding Jack's place. Iris whispered to Sunshine that Mona wanted to give her winnings to us to pay the ransom for the painting so that we didn't have to break and enter."

"What winnings?" said Amanda, with Emily's voice saying exactly the same thing in her ear. The two friends exchanged a glance.

"Her casino winnings," said Helen.

Sunshine looked at them closely. "Didn't you know?" She clasped her hands in front of her, seeming very nervous. "Iris said that Mona hit a jackpot just before this all started. She took the one-time payout of $150,000."

"I know, it boggled my mind too," she continued, her eyes bulging and her face pink, as Amanda and Emily gaped at her. "She said the money was in her new peach bag, which is wedged under the passenger seat of Iris' car."

Amanda gasped. "The money that dumped out?" She looked at Emily.

"That was from the pink bag." Emily said, back in her growly voice again. She threw up her hands in exasperation. "The one these two took from us. I knew those dratted things were going to be a headache." She turned back to the sisters. "What you say is insane. Mona was acting strangely. She must have been delusional. She would have told us if she'd won money."

"Would she Em?" Amanda shook her head. "She didn't know us from Adam. Why would she tell us about winning money?"

"She obviously told Iris, because it was Iris who told us." Sunshine was wringing her hands now.

"We understand if you don't believe us." Helen got up and stood beside her sister, looking only slightly less anxious than Sunshine. "I'm not sure I would believe us."

The four of them stood looking at one another for a moment. The breeze stirred the leaves above their heads. A car went by slowly and turned in toward the beach parking lot.

Finally, Emily broke the silence. "Oh man, we really need to find Iris. We have nothing to say about what happens to any money of Mona's. That's for the next of kin." Amanda noted that her voice held a slight edge.

Amanda nodded. "She's got a daughter somewhere. This money would be hers. Carrie's. I think her name was Carrie."

She got up and walked to the green car, opened the passenger side door and put her hand under the seat.

"There is something here."

Emily stepped up beside her and whispered in her ear. "Wait a minute, Amanda. I'm feeling a tad suspicious. Much as I like these young women, who did after all let us out and call the aid unit for Mona, we shouldn't just automatically believe them. Iris might not have said any such thing to them. They could be making up the whole story."

"True," said Amanda. "But they're right about something being hidden under here. They didn't make that up." After pulling and pushing and getting hot in the face, she finally succeeded in freeing a dusty peach bag.

"I'm afraid to open it," she said, wiping at the smudges.

"I'm not." Emily stepped forward and yanked the bag open. Two bundles of bank notes leaped into the air. "Whoa," she said, picking them up off the ground. "And there's lots more in here."

Amanda tried, but she couldn't get her mouth to close. She just stared at the many bundles of bank notes piled inside Mona's purse. She turned back to the sisters, standing between them and the money. The forest around them had gone silent. She found she now shared Emily's doubts and wondered if they should have checked for the money while the younger women were standing right here. Once again, she'd leaped before she looked. She prepared herself for another battle. Oh god, she hoped they didn't have another gun.

"You're right. There is money here. But you must understand that we cannot give it to you. We have to find Iris. This is just one more motivation to get the job done."

"Of course not," said Helen, stepping back a pace and raising her hands. "God no. We don't want you to give it to us. We didn't mean to give you that idea. That's for later, after we find Iris and take Gloria out."

Amanda relaxed slightly.

After a couple of silent minutes, Sunshine giggled. "Yes, right after we do that. How are we going to do that again?"

Helen looked around. "Should we go somewhere else? We need to plan, but maybe not while standing here by the side of the road."

***

At Starbucks they held a whispered conversation over their whipped-cream-topped mochas.

"There's one other thing Iris told us," Helen said, as soon as they all sat down. "It's a bit puzzling. Maybe you can help us figure it out. Because I think she meant it to be the most important thing. More important than the money. She came over and sat between us for a moment. She said that while everyone wanted us to get Grandmother Femke back, what you all really wanted was for us to realize that we are powerful."

Sunshine piped up. "She also said what we had to learn was how to use the power we have to stop all these bad people doing bad things to the less fortunate."

Emily burst out laughing. "And arrange world peace while you're at it."

"What power was she talking about?" asked Amanda, looking around to see if anyone was staring at them.

"We hoped you could explain," said Sunshine. "It sounded like she wanted us to be superheros or something."

"Listen to us. We're talking about her in the past tense." Helen shuddered. They all fell silent, looking sadly at one another. Then they all took sips of their coffees.

"It was strange. She said she wanted us to use the money. But she didn't want us to just pay off the thieves unless there was no other way. She wanted us to take action to stop them."

Sunshine nodded. "She seemed to have something in mind. She looked over at Mona, like she was going to bring her into the conversation, but she was asleep."

"Then Iris said, 'taking action is a great adventure, the greatest adventure you can have in life.'"

"What kind of action was she talking about?" said Emily. "You have to be careful with Iris, she gets into all kinds of scrapes entirely by accident. If her stories are anything to go by, you could head to Bellevue with the money trying to buy your picture back and end up in Ketchikan fighting off polar bears."

"Really?" Sunshine was wide-eyed.

"That's okay," said Helen. "We like adventure. It scares us, but we like it."

"We like it too," said Amanda. "Though I can do without the bears. So, Emily," she said, turning to Emily and giving her a look, "where does that leave us?"

"Fine," said Emily, with a sigh. "We'll come with you and give our evidence in your support."

"We can report Gloria's kidnapping of Iris and get the police on that, too," said Helen.

"Why didn't we think of this sooner?" said Amanda, as the last of her whipped cream melted away. "Let's go."

"I've got a feeling none of this is going to go the way we envision," said Emily, downing the last of her drink, too.

As Emily started to pull the little green car out onto the road again, Helen and Sunshine stepped toward the windows, one on each side. Emily frowned, but put her foot on the brake.

"What?" she said, rolling down the window. Amanda rolled hers down, too.

"Sunshine and I have decided that rather than wait until we get there to call the police, we're going to call them now. Give them the whole story and ask them to meet us at the casino entrance. As Amanda said, if there's something fishy going on in casino management, or security, that Gloria was mixed up in, then we can't just give the money back. It might end up in the wrong hands, and we'd have put ourselves at risk for nothing."

"We're worried about the chain of custody," said Sunshine. "I think that's what it's called."

Amanda took a hit from her inhaler, so she could speak normally. This was getting to be too much. "Report the kidnapping at the same time. Just in case, we'll stay here while you call and we can go to speaker if they want to talk to one of us." She looked at Emily. "I'm so stressed out, Em."

Emily reached for her hand. "I know, honey. But Iris will be okay. She's really tough."

Sunshine gulped. "Here goes." Helen read off the number and she tapped it into her phone.

The report didn't take long. Sunshine was put through to a detective who asked her to repeat a few things, then said he would meet them at the casino for the complete story. The faces of both sisters were ashen by the time she hung up.

Sunshine closed her eyes and took a long deep breath. "The coffee smells so good. I'd rather just stay here and have another mocha. We risk not being able to smell fresh coffee, or fresh air, for a while."

Helen laughed nervously. "Let's just get it over with."

Emily reached out the window and squeezed Sunshine's arm. "We're going to vouch for you. That should help."

"Yes, you've got four solid witnesses . . ." said Amanda helpfully. "Oh. No. I'm sorry. Three, three witnesses. If we can find Iris. I mean if Trammel hasn't . . . that is . . . we're two solid witnesses." She trailed off.

Helen and Sunshine stared at her for a moment. Amanda thought they might be reconsidering. Emily was looking at the car's ceiling. Amanda shrank back into her seat and vowed to keep quiet.

Sunshine shook it off and raised her phone. "Okay," she said, then blew out hard. "I'm doing this. I'm going to call Gloria and find out where they are."

"Be cagey though, Sun. Don't let her know anything about where we are, what we're doing." Helen turned to warn the two older women. "You two have to be silent. Silent Amanda. No matter what Sunshine says."

"We should record this," said Amanda. "How can we record?"

"Put it on speaker phone, tell her you're driving. I'll hold my phone close," said Emily.

"There's no driving noise."

Emily reached down and started the motor. "There, now there's driving noise."

Emily leaned out the window. Amanda got out and stood beside Sunshine. They all hovered expectantly as Sunshine found Gloria's listing. And they kept on hovering as her finger paused above the button. She looked scared.

"Just a second," she said, shaking her head. "It's too soon. We'll be better off to call her at the last moment so that she doesn't have time to hide. If we call too soon, we might end up warning her that something is up. Plus, by the time we go turn the money in and explain everything to the detective, she could be in Canada, or Idaho."

Helen nodded. "Good point." She turned to Emily. "What do you think? Shall we go on to the casino and meet the detective. Call her from there?"

Emily nodded thoughtfully, looking up at the sky. Amanda thought she looked like she was about to agree. Something felt wrong about this plan.

"No, you're right," Amanda said. "We should wait to call Gloria. But not until the police are there. At that point everything will be out of our hands. They might arrest you as soon as they see you and you wouldn't have time to call. Better . . ." she, too, looked at the sky for inspiration. "How about calling when we're a minute or so away from the casino? That would give you enough time to find out where she is, but not enough time for her to skedaddle."

Emily beamed at her. "Amanda, my dear, that's a brilliant alternative."

The sisters nodded enthusiastically, though their faces were still white with fear. "That's what we'll do."

CHAPTER 16

"Leverage," said Iris. She'd gathered her waning strength for another try. "I understand the concept. But I entirely miss how kidnapping me… excuse me, taking me hostage… Well to be blunt, how do I give you leverage?"

"You are the one with the most to lose. You won't do anything stupid, knowing I have your two friends and your sister captive in a place I control. Despite your surprising intuitive expertise with this technology, you will do what I say." Trammel waved the gun, still keeping it below window level. "Exactly what I say."

Except drive where you told me to go, thought Iris. But that one question still plagued her. Why was the woman so calm? Why was she sitting here, letting Iris get away with this? Was she right about what would happen in the long run?

Some other shoe had to drop eventually. If Iris couldn't stop the car until she reached the Canadian border, she would not get back in time to help her sister. How could she get to some kind of safety? Maybe she should just stop the car right here in traffic. She could cause an incident with all these witnesses. Maybe that was why Trammel was remaining calm, to keep her going until they were out of the way of all these witnesses. Iris' throat closed again. Where should she go? Not back to the house. If she could even find it. That was another problem guaranteed to make her blood pressure climb.

"The others might try to stop me, because only they themselves are at risk. People with little at stake sometimes leap into heroics before they think."

"You don't know my friends," said Iris. "Amanda has asthma. If she attempted anything heroic she'd end up wheezing on the ground. And Emily, though she's brave enough, she's very much a by-the-book kind of person. She wouldn't do anything foolish on her own. She'd just turn you in to the cops."

This wasn't helping. Iris felt her heart hammering and she needed to change the subject. She couldn't just sit here, inching along in traffic, talking about Gloria's abuses and waiting for the woman's next heinous act. She ran her mind over everything that had happened, looking for something to talk about. Something to make Gloria feel like she was on her side.

"By the way," she said, "I saw you with your friends who all had bags and they were pulling things out and showing them to the camera. Were you doing an advertisement?"

"That was a Glorious! unbagging." Gloria sounded bored. So this might not be the best topic, but now Iris was curious.

"What's an unbagging?"

"It's my branded version of an unboxing."

Well that cleared things right up. Iris smiled at the irritating woman.

"Oh."

"You have no idea what I'm talking about." Gloria smiled back at her. "It must be devastating to realize every day how out of it you really are, you poor old thing. An unboxing is a video that shows a product being opened, removed from its packaging, and displayed for the viewers who might be considering buying that product."

"What?"

"Are you deaf or slow? Someone takes a product out of its box, on camera, shows the color, or the buttons and knobs and what they do. The way it looks. How it works. So that viewers can decide whether they want that product or not. They are very popular. I get some of my highest traffic from Glorious! unbagging videos."

Iris couldn't believe her ears. Why would anyone want to watch... then she got it. She remembered, right after her husband Ken had died, when she'd not known what to do with all her free time, she'd watched something similar.

"Oh. You mean like on the Home Shopping Network." She turned to smile at her new best friend.

Gloria Trammel's eyes turned to lasers once again. Iris jumped. She could almost feel those eyes flaying the skin off of her face.

"Unbagging is nothing like the Home Shopping Network," Trammel hissed through tight teeth. "Nothing at all."

Iris tried again. "I don't know what would be different. That's where people would go to see a new type of mop being demonstrated, or a piece of jewelry on someone's wrist. It seems the same to me."

"Trust me," Gloria's voice dripped ice. "It's not the same thing at all. If you had ever taken a look at one of my videos you would know."

"Oh, well I haven't, so I don't know the difference." Iris shrugged. "It just seems like what you're describing is what I used to see on the Home Shopping Network."

"Stop saying that." Gloria was close to shouting.

Iris realized she'd made a mistake. This line of reasoning was not getting the woman on her side. She cast around for another topic.

"Do you ever do videos that help older women?" She smiled at Gloria again, as if the previous exchange had never happened. "You know, that would be a real service. Older women sometimes really need a boost in their appearance, for their confidence, as you mentioned before." She pointed to her crow's-feet. "These wrinkles for example. I'd really like to know some tricks for using makeup to minimize them."

Iris glanced Gloria's way out of the corner of her eye, then back to the road. The woman seemed to be calming down. But when she flicked her eyes that direction again again, Iris saw an evil grin spreading over the flawlessly made-up face. Gloria raised her phone. What was she doing?

"Great idea, Grandma. You're on video. We'll discuss your wrinkles."

Gloria was now completely focused on Iris' face, no longer paying any attention to where they were going, or what Iris was doing. Iris' heart did a little dance. She could do whatever she wanted now. She could get off at the next exit and drive to the police station. She knew this area relatively well. Town hall was just a couple of miles east.

A small, lime green car appeared in Iris' driver's side mirror, creeping up on her left. It caught her attention because it was the same color as her little Honda.

"Hello, my beauties," said Gloria.

"What?" said Iris, "Are you talking to my wrinkles?" As the car came along beside her, Iris realized it was exactly the same model as hers.

Gloria broke out into peals of laughter. "As you can see, I have a completely different treat for all of you today. Meet Iris. She's a few years past her prime, and a few sandwiches short of a picnic."

Iris groaned at the old joke.

"We're going to try . . ." Gloria laughed again. "And remember, in the immortal words of Yoda, try is not do . . . but we're going to try to help Iris to minimize her ugly old wrinkles. In order to lift her spirits, encourage her to be more self-confident, and, hopefully, get her to stop watching the Home Shopping Network." She laughed again. "A tall order, it's true."

Iris tried to keep her temper in check. Out the corner of her eye, she watched the little green car inch forward. She could not believe what she was seeing. Amanda sat in the front seat, a look of intense concentration on her face. On her lap she clutched a pale peach leather bag. Mona's bag. Iris' heart slithered all over the place.

What were they doing with Mona's bag? Without moving her head, Iris continued watching, glancing into the back seat as the car went by. Emily was at the wheel glowering at the road. The two of them must have been fighting about something. There was no one in the back.

Where was Mona?

Where were they going?

How had they got out of the house?

Iris laughed, and pointed toward the other side of the road. Time to pull the old lady card again.

"I'm sorry to change the very entertaining subject, but I just have to say, something is wrong with architects these days. Will you look at that thing?" She had to get Trammel to look the other direction so she could find out where Emily and Amanda were going with her car, which, she suddenly realized, they'd got out of the woods. So it wasn't damaged. That was good news, at least.

But what were they up to now? And most puzzling of all, how had they got out of that locked room?

"I think these new apartment buildings are just so ugly. Boxes jutting out all over the place. They don't make any sense."

Trammel looked briefly in the direction she was pointing, then turned back to her, one arched eyebrow raised. "As you can see friends, Iris is a very distracted driver. Perhaps she's equally as distracted about her skin care regimen. And I'm puzzled, Iris, by your idea that things should make sense. I haven't heard a single coherent word from you since I met you. Not that I expected to. We all know that old women are not the most reliable sources." She gave another sarcastic laugh.

Iris hyperventilated, forcing herself to ignore the nasty dig. The distraction had given Emily just enough time to pass and move into the lane in front of them. Now she was moving into the next lane, then the next. Her right signal still blinked. Had she forgotten about it? No, she moved over again. She was going to take the exit.

"Sorry about that digression. What were you saying about skin care?"

Ahead, a large orca whale appeared, seeming to leap above the trees. Blackfish. They were headed back to the casino. Iris blinked. And then she saw, ahead of Emily, a dark van heading off the exit ramp. That van looked very familiar. Was Emily following the sisters? What was going on? Had the young women gone back and let her friends out? But . . . Why? What? Who was in charge there? Were her friends in trouble? Amanda looked so grim. Amanda never looked grim. What was going on? She almost gasped as the realization dawned. Mona. The sisters must have Mona!

Without thinking, Iris checked all her mirrors and followed the two vehicles, squeezing in between a white cargo van and a jacked-up pickup truck.

"Oh! Oh no!" she shrieked, "something's wrong." She pressed the accelerator even harder. "Nnoooo. We're going to crash! Did you say this was a prototype?" She jiggled her knee around. "The gas!"

"There is no gas, you idiot," said Gloria Trammel, in a strained voice. She'd been momentarily knocked backward, off balance and was gripping the door handle, trying to pull herself upright against the amazing force of the silent car.

"It just keeps going and going, even when I take my foot off the pedal. Too fast! AAAAHHHH!"

Iris jerked the car into the next lane and then the next. "Look out!" With a yell of feigned and real fright, she cranked the wheel just in time to miss hitting the barrier and they jolted over the verge into the exit lane. Horns went off all around them, but Gloria Trammel, thrashing around, trying to stay upright, still managed to force the muzzle of the gun into the cleft under Iris's jawbone. It hurt, rather. Iris hoped she was catching all this on video, too.

"Whatever is happening here, it's not the fault of the car. Stop wasting my time."

A bouncy tune started playing and a woman's voice sang out, "I'm Just Upside Down." Iris screamed, then she realized it must be Trammel's custom phone ring tone.

Without slowing at all, Iris jerked the wheel again to bring the vehicle into the correct lane to follow the other two vehicles. The gun jabbed painfully and the phone flew out of Gloria's hand, smacked Iris painfully in the eyebrow and dropped between the seats.

Her eyebrow throbbed. The song played over again, and the next thing Iris knew something was trickling into her eye. Blood. The vile woman had cut her!

They flew down the road and through an intersection just as the light turned red. Silently, they scattered cars and left gaping pedestrians in their wake. Iris saw two men run out of a gas station and stand waving at the edge of the sidewalk. In the rear-view mirror, Iris saw one man had his phone to his ear. Maybe they saw what was going on inside the speeding vehicle. Though what they would make of it, she had no idea. Certainly they would report a self-driving car that was out of control. That would be the best case scenario for Iris. She kept pressing the pedal and driving like a maniac.

Gun still jammed into Iris' carotid, Gloria Trammel thrust her hand between the seats and began pawing around trying to find her phone. At least she was busy with that and not trying to get control of the car, but Iris thought she heard the woman growling. They were almost to the road that circled the casino. Surely if there were a way for Trammel to override Iris' manual control, she'd have done it by now. If she did get voice control again, Iris would have to try to counter everything she said. They'd end up shouting opposing orders at the car. How would that work? It would probably go bonkers and either drive around in circles or stop.

Preparing for the worst, Iris clamped her hands on the wheel and held on.

Trammel hadn't managed to retrieve the phone. It must have slipped down underneath the seat. She turned her attention to Iris instead. Clearly she couldn't hold the gun on Iris and reach the phone, which had stopped ringing anyway. Out of the corner of her eye, Iris saw that the woman was looking at the mode switch on top of the steering wheel. This was not going to go well. But she would let Trammel batter her and badger her any way she wanted, she was not giving up control of this vehicle while there was breath in her body.

Suddenly, with another guttural sound, the woman launched herself at Iris, her right hand a claw, nails raking at Iris' shoulder and arm. Iris bent protectively over the wheel and maintained a wide posture, fighting off Trammel's attempts to get to the switch or pull the wheel away. She had to make it to the casino. She couldn't last long under this onslaught, though. Her shoulders were beginning to give out. She had to do something. Looking around quickly, she sought anything she could use as a weapon. What she wouldn't give to have one of Amanda's knitting needles right about now. She would jab it in the woman's thigh, right through that precious pink designer skirt.

Like her sister, Mona, and every perfectly put together fashion plate Iris had ever encountered, this ostensibly smooth and polished woman went completely feral when challenged. She was all but foaming at the mouth. She bared her teeth. She growled as she clawed at Iris' fingers, trying to peel them from the wheel, then trying to push past to reach the control button. All the time she kept the gun jammed under Iris' jaw.

Why wouldn't she drop the gun? Couldn't she see that Iris was over being threatened by it? But she just kept on promising to shoot her, while Iris ignored the threat, held her head as steady as she could under the pressure of the muzzle and floored the whatever-it-was pedal.

As they caught up to her little green Honda, Iris zigged into the wrong lane and flew by, wishing she could lay on the horn, but unable to spare a hand. She zagged back into her own lane in the nick of time to avoid a head-on collision. Then she zigged back into oncoming traffic again, to go around the van.

It worked. She could see that the two vehicles had picked up speed and were trying to keep up with her. Perfect!

She had the casino entrance in sight. The van and the Honda were right on her tail. What must they be thinking? She almost breathed a sigh of relief, and then suddenly Gloria had hold of her pinky finger. Holy smoke that hurt. Iris winced in pain. That darn digit was arthritic, and painful, and not strong enough, and Gloria was working it away from the steering wheel. Iris couldn't hold on much longer. Lights began to flash in her eyes. There was a wailing ringing in her ears. She was on the verge of giving up, letting go of the wheel, passing out from the pain, when she thought of the hand sanitizer in her left pocket. Redoubling her grip of her right hand, despite the agony, she let go with her left hand and pulled out the little bottle, flipped up the cap and aimed it at Trammel's face.

There was a terrible shrieking. A direct hit! She'd squirted the vile woman right in the eye. Trammel clawed at her face, howling. Then she clawed at Iris' face and then Iris was howling, too. The stinging goo smeared across her glasses and transferred to her own eyes.

A blur appeared in front of her. Was that a car? Oh shit, she searched for the brakes. She couldn't slow down in time. She let her grip go and patted at the wheel, trying to hit the horn, then she just braced for impact and let out a cry of anguish.

Her life flashed before her eyes. Amy running across the Giant's Causeway, Ken among the flowers at Saint Michael's Mount, Bobby and her grandchildren in Hawaii. What a way to go. This was not what she'd planned at all. Though she was driving recklessly, she'd planned to drive so skillfully, nothing bad would happen. She still had to find Mona. She hadn't talked to Amy in days. Rosie was all alone at home.

Blinking, eyes stinging and streaming, Iris swerved one more time, in a final effort to avoid hitting the blur. Miraculously, she missed the other car, and equally as miraculously didn't hit anything else. Her face felt like a sheet of ice.

She closed the smeared eye and with the other was able to steal a glimpse at Trammel and almost burst out laughing.

The woman was all but embedded into her seat, pink silk bonding to black leather. She was wiping her eyes with the sleeve of her Chanel suit, the pink silk now a smeared mess. Blinking and crying, she seemed to have forgotten her still raised gun hand, which waved uselessly in midair. No time like the present, said Iris to herself. She shot out her right hand and seized the woman's wrist just as she made it to the Casino drive. Trammel yelped and fought her again.

Iris pulled the wheel just far enough to aim the car up the slight rise, then let go of the wheel and pushed the Voice Control ON button again. The car juddered. She started saying things she thought might help.

"Go around."

"Circle the fountain."

"Drive through valet parking."

She didn't know what to say to get the car to do what she wanted, she just kept spewing directions.

All the time she was gripping the wheel, fighting off Gloria Trammel's attempts to get hold of it, batting her hand away. Trying to get hold of the gun with one hand, she almost tried to steer the car with the other, then remembered that she'd put voice control back on.

She fought free of the force of habit and let go of the wheel, so she now had two hands to fight off Trammel, who was holding on with one hand, while trying to aim the gun at Iris with the other. The manic grin on her face reminded Iris of the Joker in Batman, and stripped away the last of her reservations. She wrapped both hands around Trammel's wrist and shoved it back and forth shouting, "Let go!"

The car wove, and drove in a tight circle, then went up the drive the wrong way, narrowly missing the blue van that came screeching up the drive from the other direction, straight toward them.

"Stop," shouted Iris. "Open doors."

Iris was spent. With hope fading, she gave one last feeble push at Trammel's wrist, trying to knock the gun away, but the woman was strong. Her gun hand came back toward Iris fast, and Iris felt hard metal connect with her cheekbone and a searing pain shot through her face. She lost her grip on Trammel's wrist. That was it. She was finished. The younger woman had won.

Then the support behind her disappeared and she was falling.

The gun went off.

Iris jolted to a stop, pain surged through her body, and the back of her head burst with agony. Trying to breathe, she shook herself back to reality and found she was lying on asphalt, Gloria Trammel sprawled on top of her, kicking and screaming. Looking up, Iris saw the young valet the woman had been so unkind to that morning. Was it only that morning? He was staring down at them, flanked by two other uniformed men.

What a lot of valets, thought Iris. There must be a huge crowd for Ladies' Night. And then she thought, I'm dying. She knew she was. Her chest hurt, her head hurt, she couldn't breathe. The world spun and she closed her eyes again. Trammel's bullet must have found its mark.

CHAPTER 17

Though Iris' eyes were closed, the end didn't come as she expected. She heard shouting. A car raced up and screeched to a stop nearby. Car doors opened and shut. Another vehicle arrived, and then another. She lost count.

There was a scuffling sound. Then a thwack. Someone yelled in Iris' ear and she turned away from the pain.

"We've had a report . . ." said an authoritative voice.

"You're under arrest," said another.

Someone put a hand on Iris' neck. Her eyes flew open and she prepared to go back into battle once more, despite the aches in her back and chest and the throb in her head.

Instead she saw Amanda's worried face looming over her. Emily was standing above them both holding a long blue rapier and brandishing it at the woman in pink. Both she and the woman were screaming at each other. Iris couldn't understand the words. Two cops rushed in, along with two young women. Iris moved her head, trying to take it all in, and saw two more cops laying hands on the woman in pink who seemed to be in the process of lunging for Emily's throat. Everyone was talking at the same time. Iris could make no sense of any of it.

Covering her ears, Iris struggled to sit up. Someone tried to push her back down, which just made her mad.

She shut her eyes again and screamed at them, at all of them. "Shut up! Everyone." Whoa, that hurt her throat.

Silence fell. Iris opened her eyes again and found a circle of people gaping at her. Emily still jabbed the blue sword toward the woman in pink. Iris recognized it now as Amy's telescoping walking stick. And there was Gloria Trammel, with a red welt rising on her cheek. Iris smiled to herself. She'd have to thank Amy. That really was the handiest little gadget.

The formerly beautiful and poised woman was now a wreck. Her hair had come out of its chignon and was standing on end. The red lipstick was smeared across her face even more like the Joker. But now she resembled the version played by that handsome young man who had died. What was his name? It didn't matter. All that mattered was that Trammel was in handcuffs. An officer put a hand on her tousled head to keep her from bumping it as she was loaded into the squad car. But Trammel, raging at him for daring to touch her, pulled away from his hand and in the process, bumped her head anyway.

Iris felt a surge of happiness and victory. Beside her she heard Amanda gasp and Emily laugh.

"That's a fitting exit for that bitch," said Emily. "High five, Iris." Iris raised her palm to meet Emily's. "You brought her in, laid her out and wrapped it up. This calls for a celebration. It's after eight o'clock and it's still Ladies' Night. Let's go get those free drinks and toast to the end of Gloria Trammel."

Iris tried to nod, but it hurt too much and she stopped. She struggled to sit up and Amanda grabbed her arm to help, but just then a police officer came over, pulled out handcuffs, and again said, "You're under arrest." So instead, she passed out.

CHAPTER 18

Clad in a new, lavender silk dress and matching jacket, Iris Winterbek admired herself in the mirror, turning this way and that as she smoothed the beautiful fabric. She looked pretty good for an old lady.

She'd tried a new stylist this morning and was very pleased with the result. Her hair shone with sunny glints of color. The bruise on her cheek had faded. It was hardly visible now under her makeup. The scar where Gloria Trammel's phone had split her eyebrow was still pink. She'd decided to wear it as a badge of honor.

"You look fabulous, Mom. I like the new glasses. Did you get those from Gloria Trammel?" Amy laughed and snapped another picture as Iris turned around. "Hey! You didn't even blink. Being a superhero sure suits you."

Iris smiled for another photo. She hadn't felt this good in years.

"Hi, Emily! I'm just calling to let you know the limo has arrived. Isn't it exciting? Amy is going to take my picture, and then we'll come pick up you and Amanda."

Iris paused, then continued. "I wish she were, too. She would have loved all this attention. She always did want to be treated like a queen... One toast? I say we drink a whole bottle of champagne in her honor."

Rosie trotted around Iris' feet as she headed to the back door and stepped into her bags. Amy laughed at her again, but she didn't care. Superheroes had to keep their duds looking good, and these were brand new shoes.

The day was glorious. All her chrysanthemums, marigolds, dahlias and other fall flowers were blooming. The air was fragrant and the sky was blue.

All was well in Iris' world. Except she missed Mona. A tiny tear formed at the corner of her right eye. She dabbed it away.

Most everything had turned out the way Mona wanted it to. Iris smiled again. Mona always got her way. There only remained the matter of a small painting.

"Speaking of pictures, Mom," Amy said as Iris came back into the foyer where the smiling limo driver was now standing beside her. "I'm surprised you hung that gruesome photo in the entryway."

"I don't know why," said Iris, reaching out to wipe a speck of dust off the black and white photo of herself staring straight into the camera. "I'm quite used to seeing terrible pictures of myself." This did qualify as a terrible picture, if you were looking for glamour, but Iris had been interested in something else this time. Hair tangled, eyebrows knit, mouth set in a sneer, brow bloody, and eyes blazing, she was holding a reader board with her name and the date of her arrest. "I'm very proud of my mug shot. It shows me at my very best. And anyone trying to break in needs fair warning that a bad ass lives here."

Amy rolled her eyes, the limo driver smiled a little nervously, and the three women walked out to the driveway. Iris began to pose with the uniformed young woman beside the open door of the limousine.

"Oh, wait!"

She quickly bent over and ripped the plastic bags from her feet as Amy laughed at her again from behind her camera. No doubt her incorrigible offspring would send snaps of all this foolishness to her brother. But Iris just laughed, because for the second time in her life, she didn't fear looking like the fool. Once again, she'd managed the impossible and emerged victorious.

As the limo entered the circular drive to Blackfish Casino's grand entrance, the three friends looked at one another.

"I'm nervous," said Amanda. She breathed deeply a couple of times, but didn't reach for her inhaler. Iris was proud of how quickly she was learning other coping skills.

"This is so energizing," said Emily.

Iris reached for both her friends' hands and gave them each a squeeze.

"Look," said Iris, "there's our favorite valet. He's looking very spiffy today." She jumped up, poked her head through the sunroof, and waved to the uniformed young man.

"Who are all these other people?" said Emily. "It looks like the whole staff of the casino and hotel are here. Along with the tribal elders and the town council."

There were a thousand gold balloons tied in clusters to pots of flowers, and a banner over the entry that read, "Thank You, Emily, Iris, and Amanda!" Several people held big bouquets of flowers.

"This is the most exciting thing that's ever happened to me," said Amanda, patting her own cheeks.

"More exciting than getting kidnapped in the back of a van?" said Emily.

"More exciting than a high-speed chase with a blackmailer in a self-driving car? More exciting than helping the police round up boxes of stolen cash?" said Iris.

"Well, I mean exciting in a good way," said Amanda, taking a hit from her inhaler.`

As they alighted from the car, the band started playing "Luck Be a Lady Tonight" and Iris began to laugh.

Two women stepped out of the crowd and came toward them, looking a little shy.

"Look," said Emily. "Sunshine and Helen are here, too."

"You look beautiful, girls," said Amanda to the sisters, who were wearing similar, but not matching, dark dresses. "Like ladies, without those awful security guard outfits."

"They didn't lock you up?" asked Emily, embracing one of the young women. Iris could never remember which was which.

"We made bail, thanks to Mona. Sunshine and I still have to face some charges, but we're cooperating with the police," said Helen, the brunette.

"But our attorney says we'll probably just get a lot of community service," said Sunshine.

"I'm so glad you're here." Iris put her arms around them both. "Alright ladies, let's get the party started."

"Hold on," said Amanda. "What about the painting? Did you get it back?"

The sisters looked at one another.

"That will take a while," said Helen.

"We don't have enough money now that we paid our bail," Sunshine added.

They all looked at one another. "I wondered how that would go," said Iris trying to hide her smile.

A tall, gray-haired man in an impeccable suit came toward them, arms outstretched, and the sisters melted away into the crowd.

"Ladies," he boomed, "welcome back to Blackfish. On behalf of the casino and the tribe, I extend our deepest thanks for your heroism."

The chief went on praising the three friends, while three young women in tribal dress came forward with bouquets for each of them. Photographers snapped their pictures and then the casino executives gathered around and presented them each with lifetime Gold Cards.

"Whoopee," said Amanda. "We can play those slots for the rest of our days!"

"Not that we have all that many of them," said Emily.

Amanda threw up her hands. "Emily, for heaven's sake! Don't be such a downer."

"Killjoy," said Iris, digging her friend in the ribs with her elbow.

Emily laughed.

After the photo op, they were ushered inside to Blackfish, the casino's world-class restaurant, and seated in the places of honor at a big circular table.

"This is the fanciest restaurant I've ever been in," said Emily, as a waiter poured champagne into all their glasses.

It was indeed a fancy restaurant. There were too many pieces of crystal stemware on the table for Iris to count. The silver flatware gleamed, the chandeliers were a fanciful melange of cedar bark, crystal, oyster shell and what looked like bones.

"Bosh," said Iris. "You were an executive at the biggest corporation in the Seattle area."

"I didn't do that much eating out. I just worked."

"Typical," said Amanda. "Personally, I've been to all the four and five-star places on the West Coast. So I'm very comfortable here."

"Really?" said Iris. Emily froze, glass halfway to her lips and stared.

Amanda shrugged. "Art collectors like to meet in nice places."

Iris had to admit, Amanda was shining tonight. She could really dress well when the occasion suited her. Her black silk sheath was simple, but she wore some silver and aquamarine earrings that were the creation of a first-rate silversmith. She carried a hand-painted and beaded clutch purse that, likewise, could have been in a gallery. Her makeup was perfect and her hair almost stylish. If Iris didn't know it had been taken down, she'd think Amanda had been watching the Gloria! YouTube channel.

The glow of success extended to Emily, too. While her black suit and leather briefcase-style bag were far more businesslike, she had also opted for very special earrings. The large pearl and diamond drops had surprised Iris at first, and then after a moment, came to seem just perfect.

Across the room, Iris spotted Sunshine and Helen again. The sisters were standing to the side and seemed nervous. She stood and waved them over. "Come join us."

After a round of greetings and reports of how everyone was doing, Sunshine looked at Emily and gave her a sly smile. "When you were over the other day, we forgot to ask you, Emily. How did you feel the day after Ladies' Night?"

"Oh, you don't want to know," said Emily, shaking her head, and looking a little green. "I wish I could say I didn't remember, but I'm afraid I do."

Sunshine, Helen and Amanda all laughed. Iris watched them, bewildered.

"You did Ladies' Night? I thought you got arrested."

"Not right away," said Helen. "Gloria screamed about us a lot, but we hadn't done anything. The police investigated her story first. So we were free that first night."

"If they'd looked in the van it would have been a different story," Sunshine broke in with a theatrical shiver. But Gloria was being so horrible they just wanted to get her away. She even snarled at all her ans who were gathered around trying to vouch for her. She just laughed and called them terrible names, saying they were gold digging bimbos, pathetically hanging on her every word. Of course a few of them wanted to tear her apart for saying such things to them. With all the distraction, we got lucky."

"After we gave our statements the officer dropped us back here to get our cars, so . . ."

Helen saw the look on her face and took pity on her. "Didn't you hear the story, Iris?"

"I'm not surprised Emily neglected to say anything," said Sunshine. "but Amanda, didn't you tell Iris about it?"

"What the heck happened?" asked Iris.

"Oh, you know, we were feeling pretty high on our accomplishments," said Emily, turning a little pink. "That's all."

"We?" said Amanda. "Who is this we you speak of?" She turned to Iris, but pointed at Emily. "Emily here felt rather high on her accomplishments. Since we had rooms already we stayed, rather than go back to our empty houses. That felt anticlimactic after all we'd been through that day. Not having had enough of trying new things, decided that her free Ladies' Night drinks would be those new-fangled ones the kids like. The ones they make with Red Bull."

"The energy drink?" Iris gasped. "That stuff can mess you up."

"It can indeed," said Helen. "Especially when you drink four of them. We ran after Emily all night, pulling her out of traffic, coaxing her off high ledges, agreeing with her political speeches, trying to get her to sing a little more quietly."

"Emily sang?"

"It was quite the night," Sunshine was laughing.

"Where was I?" asked Iris.

"That was while you were in the hospital being stitched up and watched for signs of concussion."

"Oh, right. That night. I was completely bored, and you were out raising hell without me."

Emily crossed her arms and raised an eyebrow. "Iris, you have never raised hell in your life."

"Well, it's time I started. I'm done with being old and acting my age. I've quit being who I once was. I used to play on a baseball team. I used to run every morning. I don't know why I stopped."

Emily snorted. "I think it has something to do with knee joints."

Helen laughed. "I realized you have more going on than I'd assumed at first glance, when I came into that bedroom and you threw me to the ground. You had martial arts training once, didn't you?"

"Yes, I did, way back in the '70s when it was all the rage for women to learn self defense. Actually, after Amy brought me home from the hospital, I called and signed up for some Tai Kwon Do classes. I meant to tell you that, Emily. Would you like to go with me?"

"I want to go with you." Amanda was almost shouting, and jumping up and down in her seat. "I've been walking every morning down to the local elementary school and teaching art classes. After what we went through, I realized I'd been way too willing to sit around and get ready to die. I'm going to go back to being who I was before all the marketing about what it means to be old got hold of me."

"That's wonderful, Amanda. And you're absolutely right, we have to keep on being who we are. We can't give up and become some archetype of what the world thinks old people should be. Though I don't think I'm going to start running again. I gave that up when my joints started to feel the strain and I'm perfectly happy to move to something a little gentler. I'll get you signed up too."

"Something gentler. Like martial arts," said Helen, and they all laughed again.

The waiter arrived and for the next few minutes they chitchatted, drank their champagne and ordered dinner.

"Wait," said Iris, turning to the sisters. "You said something earlier about being over the other day. Over where?"

Sunshine put down her glass. "Amanda and Emily dropped by on Friday and helped us put our house back together."

"We went for coffee like usual, after water aerobics," Emily said. "But we decided to get it at that new place in the Snohomish historic district. And since we were so close to their house, we got coffee for them, too."

"I love that place!" said Iris. "Why didn't you invite me?"

Amanda laughed. "We would, if you'd stayed home long enough."

Iris stopped, confused. "Hold on. Why didn't I go to water aerobics on Friday?"

"Focus, Iris," Emily said with a barking laugh. "You were in California for the weekend, visiting your son and grand kids.

"Oh. Right. Never mind me. I thought you were leaving me out of the fun, but it's just my memory acting up again."

"I don't know about fun. All you really missed was hanging curtains and unwrapping china," said Sunshine.

"I took some pictures," said Emily, "to give to the police."

"Oh," Sunshine said, jumping a little, "speaking of pictures, I saw part of the video from Gloria's phone. It was so exciting, You were so brave Iris. She filmed herself laughing at you, and threatening you. At one point I could see the gun in her hand. She was pointing it right at you!"

"Yes, she's not a very nice person, I'm afraid," said Iris.

Amanda drew herself up to her tallest, and most indignant. "Did you know she made these poor girls live out of boxes so that they would always look like they were moving and could more easily hide her money? I swear, that woman. Talk about mean."

"But she's getting her reward for her bad behavior now," said Iris. "I hope she gets twenty years."

"I'd love to visit her in prison and see her without her makeup and designer suits," said Helen.

"I wonder how she looks in orange?" said Emily. "Do you suppose she'll start a prison beauty channel?"

The five women laughed and raised their glasses. First they toasted Mona, then Iris. Amanda and Emily had their turns, too. Then the three older women drank a toast to Helen and Sunshine, though the young sisters denied having done anything.

"Nonsense. You were absolutely key. In fact, you made the whole thing possible," said Iris. "If you hadn't gone back to the house and released Emily and Amanda . . . and Mona . . . and decided to return the money, I'd just have been a crazy old woman accusing a pillar of the community of blackmail. I thank you from the bottom of my heart.

"And I especially appreciate you trying to help Mona. We know now that no matter what we did it would have been too late." She choked up and it took her a moment to get control. Amanda rubbed her back and Helen patted her hand. "I . . . uh . . . talked to her doctor. He told me he was amazed at my story. He said there was no way she should have been able to do the things she did that day. According to the hospice staff, she left without telling anyone. They'd given her only days to live, but she arranged an Uber, then spent the last of her funds to get a ticket to come see me in hopes I'd help her connect with her daughter before she died."

Iris paused for a moment and watched the bubbles rise from the depths of her glass.

"I feel terrible that I didn't listen to her right away. I didn't take time to notice how sick she was. I just dragged her off to the casino. No wonder she kept holding onto her head. She was barely able to function."

Amanda shook her head. "You couldn't know, Iris. She seemed okay. Not perfect, but okay."

"She did. She even went for coffee and meals with us, but the doctor said she hadn't been able to swallow in the last week."

"But she ate the sandwich I brought her," said Amanda.

"No, she didn't. I found it in the door pocket of the car a few days ago when I took it to the car wash."

"Did you ever speak to her daughter?" asked Helen.

"Yes, I called Carrie. She was very sad to hear her Mom had been trying to get hold of her before she passed. Though she was also a little skeptical. They never had a great relationship. She's going to come out for the funeral next week. You can all meet her then."

A silence dropped over the group. They nodded and mumbled sentiments like, "Of course. That will be nice. Looking forward to it."

After a moment, Iris leaned forward and dropped her voice. "Okay, that covers the praise for past action, and the recap of all that's happened since Gloria's capture," she said. The others leaned forward in order to hear. "It's time to move on to our next mission. Let's talk about Plan B for Grandmother Femke."

"There is no time like the present," said Emily to Sunshine and Helen, nodding. "We've done our reconnaissance and tonight is the night."

"What does that mean?" asked Sunshine, warily.

Helen pursed her lips and blanched. "You've already made a plan?"

Amanda nodded vigorously.

Sunshine put her hands over her ears. "I don't think we should hear about this. We need plausible deniability. I think that's what it's called. For our parole. Or do I mean probation?"

"No worries," said Iris. "We thought of that. Squirrel Team Three has it under control." She looked to her right and left, nodding at Emily, then Amanda. "Right, ladies?"

Emily nodded curtly. Then she smirked and pulled up the sleeve of her dress, revealing a snug, black sleeve with a thumb hole. "Got my technical duds on under my fancy dress. I'll lose the sparklers when the time comes." She jiggled her head so her earrings caught the light.

Amanda twinkled and chuckled, then said, "Oh," and moved her bag between herself and Iris. She looked around furtively, then reached inside and partially drew out a black balaclava. "I'm all set, too," she whispered, then she wheezed and stuffed the hood back in her bag.

"I'm not going to be so shy." Iris whipped out her Lone Ranger mask, strapped it on her face, and raised her glass to the group. "I'm done being shy, and risk-averse, and adventure-phobic . . ."

Amanda gasped.

Emily said, "Oh, Iris, for heaven's sake."

Sunshine and Helen started to giggle and they both put their hands over their mouths.

"Humpf," said Emily. "A little party mask is not the epitome of bravery in my book. What I want to know is, have you given up wearing plastic bags on your feet when you take the dog out? That's my gauge of whether you've let go of your anxieties."

Iris reddened. "Well, actually, I am still pretty germophobic. And . . . yes, I do still battle my fear of taking risks." She looked around at each of them. "But you get the idea, right? I mean, here I am in public with a crazy mask on, making a fool of myself, which I do often, but this time it's on purpose."

"We certainly do, Iris. We've seen you in action, we know what you can do, and we applaud your effort," said Amanda. The others nodded, even Emily.

"So, in honor of my belatedly beloved sister Mona, who very much wanted these young women to get their painting back, I'm on to the next adventure – the rescue of Grandmother Femke." She jumped to her feet.

"Hi-ho, Squirrels, away!"

Ignoring the stares of the diners around them, the other four women rose and raised their glasses to meet Iris'. As their glasses clinked together, they shouted, "Squirrel Team!" and then laughed until they couldn't stand up any longer.

Just then, the waiter arrived with their dinner.

And it was still hot.

ABOUT THE AUTHOR

Nancy Bartlett lives and writes on a sailboat and travels every chance she gets. She has a passion for all things salt water, and a particular concern for the marine environment.

With her husband, Tom, she has cruised the entire East Coast of the US, sometimes offshore and sometimes inshore along the Atlantic Intracoastal Waterway (ICW).

Formerly a technical writer tasked with describing lasers, software, and corporate procedures, she's happier now that she spends her days dreaming up ways to get fictional people in and out of trouble. (That does not mean that the trouble they get into won't someday involve lasers, software, or an HR policy.)

Curious about the world of a live aboard novelist? Visit www.tidallife.com.

See Nancy's photos on Instagram at @tidallife.ig.

ACKNOWLEDGMENTS

Many people helped make *Iris All In what it is*.

Dorothy Yuill Taylor Hansen, my Mom, served as the model for Iris. Unable to stop at one story, I had to give her another kick ass adventure.

Tom Bartlett brainstormed the original story concept with me while hiking Ebey's Landing on Whidbey Island. Some of the crazy scenes were his idea. Here's to many more hikes and more stories.

Arlene Ehrlich, sailing friend and fellow bibliophile, served as the initial reader and provided insight for making the story better.

Lori Gudmundson went above and beyond, taking time out from her idyllic life of cruising in the Bahamas to edit the manuscript, enabling me to meet my deadline.

Ana Grigoriu-Voicu sorted through all my conflicting ideas and well-meaning input to create the cover and the series branding.

Mari, Emily, and Jeremy read early drafts, gave honest feedback, and surrounded Iris with support. I love you all.

THANKS FOR READING!

If you had fun with this book, Iris and I will be eternally grateful if you'll add a short review on Amazon, or wherever you bought the book, on Goodreads, or on your favorite book review site. This will help other readers decide if they'd like Iris' story.

You can also contact me at nancy@tidallife.com. I'd appreciate hearing from you about things you liked about Iris, questions you have about the series, or suggestions for future adventures.

Please also check out the Iris Winterbek Gallery on my website, www.tidallife.com to see some of the places that feature in these stories.

Happy Adventuring!

MORE ADVENTURES OF THE WORLD'S MOST UNEXPECTED ACTION HERO

Iris Incensed

In book one of the Iris Winterbek series, Iris and her daughter Amy are touring Europe and end up ensnared in the nefarious plot of a band of smugglers. Feisty though she may be, Iris has to dig deep to find her inner super hero and save the day.

Iris Everafter

Book three of the Iris Winterbek series finds Iris spending Christmas in Florida hiding from a Russian oligarch who is searching for his runaway girlfriend. Water phobic Iris inadvertently heading out to sea in a sailboat all by herself is only one part of the crazy chaos that follows.

Available in e-book and paperback on Amazon, Kobo, and Barnes and Noble.

ALSO BY NANCY BARTLETT

Panic In Any Other Language

Essays of travels in Italy ranging from cringe-worthy to heartfelt, but always aiming for the funny bone.

O 2 B MFK

A trio of culinary memoirs exploring the ways food – whether sweet or savory – can be a little unsettling.

The Doppler Effect

Three stories about that whooshing sound parents hear as their offspring too swiftly grow up and fly away.

All available in e-book on Amazon.com .

Made in the USA
Columbia, SC
04 February 2023

11318925R00117